The Return of Magic!

"What sort of a show are you planning, Mr. Innisfree?"

Innisfree turned and gestured broadly, waving both arms. "A grand and glorious spectacle, Arthur!" he proclaimed. "My companions and I, we call ourselves the Bringers of Wonder, and we have wonders indeed to show your sleepy little town!"

Innisfree's accent had changed yet again . . . .

THE REBIRTH OF WONDER

LAWRENCE WATT-EVANS

TOR fantasy ®

A TOM DOHERTY ASSOCIATES BOOK
NEW YORK

This is a work of fiction. All the characters and events portrayed in this book are fictitious, and any resemblance to real people or events is purely coincidental.

THE REBIRTH OF WONDER

Copyright © 1992 by Lawrence Watt Evans

Cover art by Pat Morrissey

A Tor Book
Published by Tom Doherty Associates, Inc.
175 Fifth Avenue
New York, N.Y. 10010

Tor ® is a registered trademark of Tom Doherty Associates, Inc.

ISBN: 0-812-51406-8

First edition: October 1992

Printed in the United States of America

0 9 8 7 6 5 4 3 2 1

In memory of Jack Wells

CONTENTS

THE REBIRTH
OF WONDER

Chapter One

CUE 84: *Grandmaster slow fade, count of ten, to black. Count five, and wait for the curtains to close completely; then bring up the curtain-warmer on Dimmer #3 for curtain calls.*

No problem. Art Dunham took a final glance at the cue sheet clipped to the cord of his work light, just to be sure he wasn't missing anything. Reassured, he turned his attention back to the stage, keeping his right hand closed firmly on the black knob of the largest lever.

Jamie was alone on the stage, giving the closing speech, and he'd gotten himself off-center, off his mark, so the pink light was all on the near side, and his other side was washed in blue. That was something to mention, last performance or not; Jamie meant well, and he could act, but he was so damn sloppy about the details sometimes!

". . . If we be friends . . ."

That was the cue. Still watching the stage, Art gripped the big lever more tightly and began pulling it down, slowly and steadily. It took some muscle; the controls were old and stiff, and there were half a dozen dimmers mastered on—not with electronics, like some modern boards, but with old-fashioned mechanical linkages.

". . . and Robin," Jamie said with an appropriate bow and flourish, "shall restore amends."

That was the last line; Art continued the fade. Either his count was off tonight or Jamie, eager to be done with the show, had rushed his delivery; there was an awkward

3

half-second before the lights were completely down when Jamie was standing alone on the stage, silent and motionless. That hadn't happened at any of the previous performances or rehearsals.

Please, Art thought, don't move, Jamie. Don't look over here to see what's taking so long. Don't run offstage. It would ruin the effect.

Then the lights were out, and as he reached up with his left hand for the #3 dimmer he heard Jamie scampering off the far side of the stage.

The curtains were closing, which was good; Marilyn was slow getting started, sometimes. She wasn't really big and strong enough to be working the ropes alone, but the actors had never settled on who should help her when, so Marilyn had to make do. Typical of actors, Art thought.

Applause was welling up from the audience, the first tentative patter turning into a spilling roar, like a summer thunderstorm breaking.

The curtain was completely closed, so far as Art could see from his place at the board, and he'd counted his five; he unceremoniously shoved the #3 dimmer to the top. With rustles and whispers and uneven footsteps the players slipped through the curtains at stage right and walked out to take their bows.

For perhaps the hundredth time, Art wished that the theater had proper footlights and overhead strips. The curtain-warmer he'd rigged, despite his best efforts, still left shadows where no shadows should be. He couldn't see them from backstage, of course, but he knew they were there. With the curtains closed and no strip lighting out front, just a couple of Fresnels, there wasn't a thing he could do about it—but he still resented it. It was his job not just to do the best he could with what was available, but to do the lighting *right*.

He promised himself, as he had a dozen times before, that somehow, somewhere, he would scrounge up the materials and build himself some new strips, first chance he had.

Which might be fairly soon, he thought with a rather grim satisfaction—this was the last show of the summer, and it was only the second of August.

The applause faded away, and the actors came running off the stage, smiling broadly. Art could hear the more impatient members of the audience getting up to go, their voices and the rustle of their clothing increasingly audible over the diminished clapping.

The actors, too, were talking as he pulled the #3 dimmer back down on a count of five. As it passed the halfway mark in its slot he reached up above the lighting board to the dimmer knob at the end of the bank of switches on the wall, and turned it, bringing up the houselights. He heard Anne and Susan giggling, and Jamie babbling happily about something.

When he had the houselights all the way up he slid his hand over an inch or two and flicked the ordinary toggle switch that turned on the backstage work lights, then reached up and tugged the chain that turned off his own little work light.

He left the stage unlit, though of course the backstage lights kept it merely dim instead of dark; any brighter light there might show through the curtain.

Besides, the onstage work lights had been gelled over as rudimentary strips, as usual, and they were patched through a dimmer at the moment, which was another reason to leave them off. It was time to shut down the board.

Somebody on the other side of the stage was opening a bottle of champagne; Art wished that whoever it was had waited until the last of the audience was out of the theater. That was sloppy showmanship; the popping cork must have been audible clear out to the lobby. That violated what Art considered a basic theatrical principle: that the audience out there should never be reminded that there *is* a backstage.

The pop was followed by laughter and high-pitched voices—released tension at work, now that the show was over, not just for tonight, but for good.

"Hey, Art!" someone called. "Come and get it!"

"Just a minute," Art answered, "I've got to reset the board!"

"You can do that later!"

"I'll do it now," Art replied. "I don't want to forget."

He wasn't likely to forget, really; he just hated leaving anything hanging.

He began systematically turning the knobs that uncoupled the individual dimmers from the masters, and the masters from the grandmaster, checking to be sure that each lever was pushed all the way down to zero. When he had checked everything to his satisfaction he reached up and ripped the cue sheets from the clamp that held them, then dropped them neatly into the wastebasket beside the lighting board.

Then he reached over and threw the master switch, cutting all power to and from the main board.

After a final glance around the curtain, out at the empty house, he crossed the stage toward the clustered actors and crew.

As he drew near someone patted him on the back; when he turned around to see who it was a plastic cup of champagne was thrust into his hand. He caught it awkwardly, slopping a little onto his fingers.

"It went just fine tonight, didn't it?" someone asked.

"Pretty well, I guess," Art answered absentmindedly. He caught sight of Jamie, still in costume but with his makeup smeared and half gone, and called, "You were off-center for your final speech, kid, halfway out of the light!"

"I was?" Jamie laughed. "Oh, well, maybe next year I'll get it right!"

"What about next *month*?" an unidentified female voice asked. "Has anyone heard anything?"

"No one's booked the theater," Art answered. "No one's even asked Dad about it, so far as I know."

"I didn't want to do a second show this year anyway,"

Jamie said. "I'm going out to California for a couple of weeks."

"Yeah, that's fine for you," Susan said. She had removed most of her costume and was wearing only a black leotard, without any of Titania's fairy splendor. "Some of us aren't going *anywhere*."

"I'd love to do another show, if anyone's planning one," someone said.

"So would I."

There was a general chorus of agreement, followed by a few dissenting voices.

"I guess," Art said, "that if anyone was planning one, he'd have no trouble finding a cast."

"And no trouble getting a tech crew, either—you come with the theater, don't you, Art?" It was Marilyn's voice; Art looked for her, and spotted her off to one side, near the ropes.

"When I get paid," Art agreed. "Not that I'm an entire crew."

"Oh, don't talk about money!" Susan protested.

"Why not? Just because you don't have any?" Jamie joked back.

"That's one good reason," Marilyn said.

"Well, hey, Marilyn, you could probably talk your way into a share of the profits if you wanted to get paid to work here," someone answered.

"*What* profits?" half a dozen voices asked simultaneously.

Anne's voice overrode the laughter, demanding, "Has anyone counted tonight's take yet?"

George's voice called from the men's dressing room, "I'm counting it now!"

"If there's any left, I vote we give it to Marilyn," someone said.

"No, it's gonna pay for the cast party!"

"I mean if there's any left *after* the party."

"There never is!"

"We'll make *sure* of that!"

7

More laughter ensued, continuing until George appeared in the dressing room door, cashbox in hand.

"Ladies and gentlemen!" he shouted above the hubbub. "I have an announcement!"

The cheerful babel faded momentarily into relative quiet.

"Our proceeds tonight have exceeded my expectations, and we will *not* have to take up a collection! In fact, after setting aside the balance of what we owe Art and his father, and covering all other necessary expenses, I find we have a surplus totaling seventeen dollars and fifty cents with which we are free to party!"

The babbling surged anew, and someone proposed a toast.

"To George," he called, "our director and producer, who kept the lot of us safely off the streets for the past six weeks!"

"To George!"

Two dozen plastic glasses were raised in salute, and cheap champagne was drunk or spilled. Art sipped his carefully, avoiding outthrust elbows, listening to the shouted comments.

"Hey, if we didn't have to pay Art, we'd have lots of money left!"

"Yeah, but we wouldn't have a theater or anyone to run lights."

"But maybe we could hire a new director."

"Ha!" Art said. "You'll never find a director who works as cheap as I do!"

"You love it, Art, and you know it."

"You don't care about the money!"

"Yes, I love it," Art agreed, "but yes, I care about the money, too!"

"George, do you really have to go?" Marilyn asked.

"Yes, I really do," George replied, "and you know I do. My folks have been planning this for years."

"Yeah, poor George! He has to go to Europe while all

the rest of us get to sit around and do nothing for a month!''

"I don't see why someone else can't direct," said a peevish voice.

"D'you want to try it?''

"What about producer?''

"Oh, that's easy!''

"Producer is nothing. We've got the theater right here, and it hardly takes any money . . .''

"That's what *you* think!''

"If anyone wants to volunteer to direct and produce another show this summer," Art said, "it's fine with me.''

"More money, huh, Art?''

"I thought you said you wanted a vacation, Art!''

"And it looks like I'm going to get one," he retorted. "I don't hear anyone volunteering!''

There was no answer to that. The conversation broke up gradually into several smaller conversations, none of which included Art. Two of the women were badgering George, one on either side of him, asking him to take them along to Paris. Anne and Susan and Jamie were in a corner together, laughing at each other's jokes. The other actors, and the guests they had let in, gathered in clumps of three or four, talking and laughing, while Art found a gap between ropes where he could lean back against the wall and sip his champagne.

It was very cheap champagne, that was obvious, but what else, he asked himself, could he expect from a bunch of amateurs like this? Half the cast wasn't even out of high school yet; the girls who had played Titania's attendants might still be in *junior* high. This might be the first champagne some of them had ever tasted—it could give them entirely the wrong idea of what the stuff was *supposed* to taste like.

But it was no business of his; he was part of the theater, not part of the company. It was entirely possible that he would never see any of these people again after the party broke up—and that might happen despite several sincere promises of help in striking the set and cleaning up the entire building. Somehow, such promises tended to be forgotten once the final performance was over.

For the past three years George had always made a point of helping, and he had always dragged along whomever else he could find—but he wouldn't be around this time. His flight left Sunday morning, a detail that had canceled the final matinee that had originally been planned—even if they could have managed without a director, George also played the Duke of Athens, and they'd run out of male understudies.

The early departure meant George would be unable to stay late at the cast party. The women who had been trying to get into his bed—there was always at least one, every show, attracted either by the director's aura of power, or simply by George's natural charm—would be disappointed.

If he had been in George's position, Art thought, he wouldn't have been so reluctant a conquest. He wasn't the director, though; he was just the lighting director, a fixture of no particular interest.

"Hello, Art," someone said.

He turned, and found Marilyn peering at him around a cluster of ropes.

"Hi," he replied.

"How's the champagne?"

"Awful."

"I know." She stared at him for a moment; he let his gaze wander out past her to the mob of teenaged actors and actresses, and the friends and family members who had drifted backstage to join them. They looked younger every year—not because they *were* younger, but because they stayed the same, on average, while he grew older.

The individual actors changed, and went off to other places or found other interests, but there were always new ones, always the same—and he was always here, helping out, and growing older, the gap between himself and the actors steadily widening.

"There really won't be another show this summer?" Marilyn asked. "The theater will just be empty?"

He could hear her dismay. He shrugged and sipped his champagne.

"I don't know," he said. "Something might turn up. No one's talked to my father, though."

"Why don't *you* talk to him?"

Startled, Art stared at her. "About what?"

"About renting the theater, of course!"

Puzzled, he looked closely at her, noticing that she had a black smear of something on one cheek. "About *who* renting the theater?" he asked. "Nobody wants it for the rest of August. I suppose we'll have all the usual meetings and concerts come fall, but nobody's *asked* for it for August. Not even hinted."

"Couldn't *you* rent it?"

Art studied her, baffled. "I could get it free, if no paying customers show up," he said. "I mean, my dad knows I have to come in here to clean and check the place over whether it's rented or not, so why not? But what would I *do* with it?"

"You could put on another play," Marilyn insisted. "You'd have no trouble finding a cast, you said so yourself, and I'd be glad to stage-manage and do sets and crew again."

"Oh, right," Art said. "Who's going to direct? George is going to Europe, Jack Gunderson is in Oregon, Fred Sohl is working for IBM somewhere, and Jenny Dawson's got kids to take care of. Who else in Bampton knows anything about directing?"

"*You* could do it. Or we could do it together."

Art shook his head. "I don't know anything about directing, and I don't want to."

Hesitantly, Marilyn ventured, "Then I could direct, maybe."

"If you want to try doing it yourself, go ahead; I'm sure my father will be easy to persuade. He hates to have property standing empty. Don't expect anything from me,

11

though, beyond what I always do—I'll hang and run your lights, and I'll handle building maintenance, and that's it. That's my job.''

"You won't help me direct?''

"Nope. Get someone else.'' He waved his almost-empty cup at the crowd of half-costumed, smiling people.

"They're just kids,'' she said.

"So?''

"You've been here for years, Art. You probably know more about putting on a play than anyone else here, even George.''

"I just run lights,'' Art insisted.

"But you've been here for every show I remember! You've watched how everything is done, you must want to try something besides lighting!''

He shook his head. "Nope. Not really. I've been here running lights for the last ten years because it's something to do in the summer, a way to pick up a few bucks and help out my dad, but that's about it. I never wanted to act or direct any more than most of those kids wanted to run lights. I've stayed on here because my father doesn't trust anyone else not to burn the place down, that's all.''

"But then what will you *do* all summer?'' she asked, her tone almost desperate.

"Oh, I don't know—spend some time at the beach, read a few books, or see a lot of movies. Just relax, that's what I intend to do.''

She stared at him for a moment, then lowered her eyes. "I guess it's different for you. You're not going anywhere. I'm going off to grad school in September, though, and I hate to waste my last month in Bampton.''

"You'll be back sometimes, won't you?''

"Yes, but . . . oh, hell.'' She turned away from him and shuffled off.

He watched her go, then shrugged and looked for more champagne.

Chapter Two

NOBODY HAD showed up to help him strike.

Art was not surprised at all. George was somewhere over the Atlantic by now, well on his way to his parents' dream vacation in Europe, the whole clan reunited in London and Paris. The others had all forgotten, or were still sleeping off the party, which had lasted deep into the morning, roaring on long after George had gone off to bed (alone).

Art considered phoning a few people and demanding that they come and help, but decided against it. He didn't think he wanted to see a bunch of bright and cheerful young faces—or even dirty, sullen ones, so long as they were that young. Bampton Summer Theatre's rental contract said the group was required to leave the premises clean, and at least as tidy as it was when they arrived in June, but nobody, not even Art's father, who owned the place, ever seemed to take that clause seriously. Cleaning up was Art's job—and unpaid, except in the form of continued free lodging in his father's house.

That meant he had to do the job alone, and the larger pieces of the sets would have to just sit in the wings for now; they were too big and awkward for one person to haul down to the basement for storage.

The first priority, though, before striking the set or any of the other equipment, was to clean up the party debris.

Art had come prepared, with half a dozen green plastic trash bags and a pocket full of twist-ties. He gathered up the cups and napkins and empty bottles and tossed everything in the bag—he was not going to worry about sorting anything for recycling. If someone wanted to sort through the bag later, that was fine with him, but he wasn't about to do it himself.

13

When the trash was collected from the stage and wings he tackled the tiny dressing rooms and lavatory, and finally the house.

He was scraping up a pink wad of relatively fresh chewing gum from the aisle floor, two rows from the back, when he heard the theater's big front door rattle. Startled, he froze where he was kneeling, then looked up at the lobby doors.

He heard voices. He put down the putty knife and dustpan and stood, brushing the dust from the knees of his jeans.

"I think you'll see that it's bigger inside than it looks," Art heard through the door. He relaxed; the voice was his father's.

"Oh, I saw that last night," an unfamiliar voice boomed, a voice with a slight British accent. "I was here for the play, for *A Midsummer Night's Dream*. A fine show they put on, a fine show!"

Art grimaced slightly. The show had been okay, but nothing special, even for a bunch of amateurs.

The lobby doors were locked; Art stepped up and threw back the bolt just as his father turned the knob from the other side. Together they swung the double doors wide.

"Art!" his father greeted him. "Glad you're here. This is Mr. Innisfree—he says he might be interested in renting the theater for the rest of August. Mr. Innisfree, this is my son Arthur."

Mr. Innisfree was a tall thin man with curly brown hair, his face darkened by sun and creased by lines left by smiles. He was wearing a broad-brimmed straw hat, white shorts, and a long, loose white shirt that looked vaguely North African—appropriate garb for the weather, which was hot, even for August, by New England standards. His age was hard to guess, but Art judged it to be at least twice his own twenty-six years.

The hair, Art thought, was probably dyed.

Mr. Innisfree shook Art's hand vigorously and said, "Arthur—that's a *fine* name, for a fine young man!"

"Thank you, sir," Art replied. "Call me Art."

"I will, my lad, I will. So this is your theater?" He surveyed the hall.

"It's a fine building," Art said loyally.

Mr. Innisfree grinned broadly. "I'm sure it is, Arthur," he said, spreading his hands. "I'm sure it is!"

It seemed his accent had changed slightly; where before Art would have thought he was English, now he sounded Irish. The lilt wasn't strong enough to be certain either way.

The elder Dunham gestured sweepingly. "Seats three hundred," he said.

Art quirked a corner of his mouth, and did not point out that the place could only seat three hundred by using every single seat, including the ends of the front row where most of the stage could not be seen, and the dusty old balcony that was now largely taken up with sound equipment and an empty projection booth.

Mr. Innisfree nodded, smiling.

"Would you like to see backstage?" Art asked.

"Yes, lad, I would," Mr. Innisfree said, his accent now almost a Scottish burr.

The three men marched down the center aisle. "I'm afraid I haven't finished cleaning up," Art apologized.

"Of course not," Innisfree replied. "Who'd have expected it? I shan't be troubled by a little dust."

"Well, it's not dust so much," Art explained. "I mean, the lights are still set up, and the flats are still hung, and the sets aren't put away . . ."

"Don't worry about it, young Arthur!" Innisfree told him, as he vaulted onto the stage. "We'll take care of everything!"

Art smiled briefly at the sight of a man Innisfree's age hopping like that; there were high school kids he knew who didn't have that much energy.

"Oh, you don't have to do that," Art's father hastened to say, as he made his way around to the stage-right steps.

"We'll take care of cleaning the place out for you and getting it ready for your show."

"Uh . . ." Art hesitated, still standing in the "orchestra pit," then asked, "What sort of a show are you planning, Mr. Innisfree?"

Innisfree turned and gestured broadly, waving both arms. "A grand and glorious spectacle, Arthur!" he proclaimed. "My companions and I, we call ourselves the Bringers of Wonder, and we have wonders indeed to show your sleepy little town!" Innisfree's accent had changed yet again, to something Art couldn't place that was still vaguely British. He wondered whether these shifts meant the man was completely phony.

Probably born in Brooklyn, Art thought.

"Oh?" he said politely.

"Yes, indeed!" Innisfree said. "We intend to stage our first production of that mystical classic of the stage, *The Return of Magic*, here, before we take the show on the road. One show and one show only, on the thirtieth of August."

Art blinked. *"The Return of Magic?"* he asked.

"That's right, Arthur—right here in Bampton, Massachusetts, we will put on such a production as the world hasn't seen in centuries!"

Arthur climbed up onstage before replying, "I'm not sure this theater has the facilities for a big production, Mr. Innisfree. I mean, this isn't exactly Broadway."

"No fear, lad," Innisfree answered, looking about with interest, his gaze taking in the inadequate flies, the ancient and rusty lightboard and patch cords, the slightly frayed ropes and somewhat musty curtains, the peeling, oft-painted dressing room doors. "I'm not seeking Broadway, nor off-Broadway, nor off-off-Broadway, to as many offs as you might choose; there's nothing broad about the way we follow. Ours is a narrow path of experiment, a route full of curious twists and unknown byways, not the flamboyant and gaudy displays that tourists attend."

"Well, then, I'm sure that this theater will do just fine," Art's father said, forcing a smile.

"And I am, too," Innisfree replied.

"Then all we need to do is settle the terms of the lease," Dunham *pére* said, his smile a little more genuine now. "One month, correct?"

Innisfree nodded, then stared up at the catwalk high overhead.

"Rent is five hundred dollars, plus you'll be responsible for the electric bill—I don't think we need to worry about heat in August. Water is included—they only bill quarterly anyway, so it's not worth breaking it out."

"Indeed it's not," Innisfree agreed, tugging gently at the curtain.

"Art, here, can handle lights and cleanup—he usually gets six dollars an hour, but that's between you. And he knows all the locals—he can get you whatever other help you need."

"Oh, we shan't need him," Innisfree said, turning back to the Dunhams. "Or anyone else local. We'll take care of our own lights."

The elder Dunham, taken aback, paused for a moment before asking, "Well, what about sets? Costumes?"

Innisfree smiled at them. "Sets, costumes, cast, director, dancers, stagehands, roustabouts, janitors, music, lights, darks, sound and silence, we'll take care of it all, Mr. Dunham!" he announced.

Art's father glanced at Art, who shrugged.

"I don't know," Dunham began.

"*Mister* Dunham," Innisfree said, "our little group is a selective one, and our preparations are private—you might even say secret, hidden, occult, cryptic. While I'm certain Arthur here is a fine young man and the very soul of discretion, we'd really prefer to take care of ourselves and clean up our own messes. A closed set, as it were."

Dunham's mouth tightened.

"No," he said. "I'm sorry, Mr. Innisfree, but this is an old building, and it's got its delicate features, its little quirks. There's a lot of valuable property in here, too, and these old wooden buildings—no. I'm not just offering Art

17

as a favor to anybody; he's my agent here, and I won't rent to you unless he's in here every day that your people are. He knows this place better than anyone else, better than *I* do. I don't want anyone else setting lights in here, I want someone who will keep an eye on things like smoking, and any fire effects you use in your show—it's too easy to start a fire in a theater, especially an old wooden one like this. And that catwalk up there, the locks and storerooms—no. I want Art in here regularly, and I want him inspecting anything you do with the wiring, and nobody uses the lighting equipment without his okay."

Innisfree stared at him for a moment, but Dunham's expression remained firmly set. Finally, Innisfree sighed.

"Very well," he said. "Your son will be free to come and go, and we'll pay him for his time—but we won't be making much use of his skills."

Dunham looked at Art.

"That's fine," Art said. "I don't mind a rest."

"Good enough then!" Innisfree grinned and thrust out a hand. "Shake on it, and the pact is made, the bargain set!"

They shook, while Art watched.

Ten minutes later they were back at the office of Dunham Realty; the paperwork was settled in short order, and Innisfree put down the required deposit in the form of a cashier's check drawn on a Boston bank. The two older men shook hands again, and Innisfree turned to go.

"Wait a minute," Art called. "When should I meet you there?"

Innisfree turned back. "Tomorrow morning at eight? Would that be too early?"

Art shrugged. "That would be fine," he said.

"Then at eight it shall be. We'll meet in the lobby, shall we?"

"If you get there first, we'll meet out back," Art said. "I still have the keys—I need to get in there to finish cleaning." He held up the ring and rattled it. "Try the back door—if I get there first I'll leave it open. The stage door, I mean."

"As you say, then," Innisfree agreed. "In the lobby at eight."

Art frowned, but didn't bother to correct him again. Instead he just watched him go.

When he stepped out onto the sidewalk himself and headed back down Thoreau Street toward the theater, Innisfree was nowhere in sight.

Chapter Three

IT WAS almost midnight by the time Art was finally satisfied with the theater's readiness for its new tenants. He had everything as clean as he could reasonably get it, working single-handed. The ropes were all coiled away, in two neat rows; the lighting instruments were ungelled and stored away on the stage-left shelves, licos on top, Fresnels below. The gels, frames, cords, and plugs were sorted and put away as well, the onstage work lights stripped back down to ordinary hundred-watt bulbs, their power routed back through the regular wall switches.

The sets were disassembled, the pieces either back in basement storage or, if they were too big for him to manhandle downstairs alone, arranged along the back wall of either wing.

The dressing rooms were swept and emptied, the costumes back down in the basement, in wardrobe storage; the ashtrays were dumped and wiped, the toilet scrubbed.

In the house the seats were all brushed, litter removed, the floor swept. Posters had been removed from the lobby walls, the red runner was hung over the fence out back to be beaten, and the two burnt-out bulbs in the lobby chandelier had been replaced.

No one from the cast of *Midsummer Night's Dream* had shown up except Marilyn. Of course, she was technically crew, rather than cast, Art corrected himself; none of the cast ever came.

Art hadn't really expected Marilyn, either, but she had arrived late in the afternoon and apologized for not being there sooner—family business had kept her away.

Marilyn's help made the job considerably easier. Art had even considered taking advantage of her presence to haul the rest of the sets down to the basement—the mock stage for "Pyramus and Thisbe" was the big one, and then the two sections of Titania's bower were awkward—not all that heavy, but awkward.

He had put it off, however, as being of secondary importance, and Marilyn had had to leave at eleven, so the sets still sat in the wings when he locked up and went home to bed.

He was in bed by 12:30, with the alarm set for 7:00, and he was up again at 6:50; he had always hated alarm clocks, hated having any machine ordering him around and telling him he wasn't doing what he should, and he had long ago developed a defense mechanism against them—he always woke up before they went off.

A warm shower, then breakfast, and then down the street to the theater, arriving at ten to eight—plenty of time. He fished the key ring out of his pocket and let himself in the front, with the intention of taking a quick look around, just in case he'd missed anything, before opening the stage door for Mr. Innisfree.

The interior was dim; sunlight spilled in the door around him, and dust, stirred up by his cleaning the night before, danced in the golden air.

"Ah, good morrow to you, lad!" Mr. Innisfree said.

Astonished, Art jerked away from the door and turned to stare.

Innisfree was standing on the left-hand balcony stair, wearing a light gray suit and smiling down at him.

"How'd you get in here?" Art demanded.

"Why, the door was open!"

"It was?" Art turned and stared. "No, it wasn't; I just now unlocked it."

"Not that one, my boy, the stage door."

Art frowned. He had locked all the doors last night when he left, hadn't he? He had certainly thought so.

He remembered checking the front doors before he walked home, and taking a look down at the big basement door, where the chain and padlock had been securely in place. He had come out through the stage door—was it possible he hadn't locked it behind him?

He *thought* he had locked it . . .

"We found it open when we arrived, so we came inside to look around," Innisfree added, helpfully.

"We?"

"Certainly, we; didn't I tell you? Did you think I was alone? I'm *sure* I mentioned the others; after all, what would one man do with a theater?"

"I knew you had a group," Art admitted. "The Harbingers of Wonder, or something like that? But I didn't know you were . . . I mean, I thought you'd be coming alone this morning, to sort of plan things out before the others got here."

"By no means, Arthur!" Innisfree smiled broadly. "Ours is a cooperative effort, and we must all *share* in the planning, if our little production is to have the success we hope for!"

Art nodded.

"Oh, and it's the *Bringers* of Wonder, not harbingers," Innisfree added.

The door to the house opened just then, and a face appeared between the two valves of the big double door. It was no one Art had ever seen before, a rather tall, thin woman, obviously Oriental—in fact, without knowing exactly why he thought so, Art classified her specifically as Chinese. She was wearing a long, utterly simple white dress—the sort of simplicity that dress designers charged a fortune for. She wore her hair long—lush, straight black

21

hair that spilled past her waist, so fine that it seemed to float about her in a cloud.

And she was staggeringly beautiful.

"Ah, Ms. Fox!" Innisfree called. "Come on out here and meet young Arthur Dunham, our landlord's scion and representative!"

The name Fox was hardly Chinese—but then, it wasn't Asian at all. "Hello," Art said.

Ms. Fox emerged two tentative little steps into the lobby and then bowed, without making a sound.

Art blinked. He couldn't remember anyone bowing to him before, ever, and was unsure how to respond.

Then Ms. Fox whirled and vanished back into the theater's depths; the sudden motion sent her hair up into a glorious black cloud, and perfume spilled from it into the surrounding air. Art took a step after her, then looked up at Innisfree.

Innisfree smiled. "Go on in, lad, and meet the others!"

Art was getting tired of being called "lad" or "my boy"—after all, he was twenty-six years old, he wasn't a kid.

This wasn't the time to argue about it, though. He went on into the theater.

The others were up on the stage, milling about and speaking quietly among themselves; most of them were smiling. As Art watched, Ms. Fox leaped up to rejoin them, jumping the thirty vertical inches as if it were nothing.

There were about a dozen, and at first he saw them as an undifferentiated mass. Gradually, though, individuals emerged.

To one side, crouched against the proscenium, fingering the ancient velvet of the curtain's edge, was a bent old woman, her white hair straggling out around a red kerchief; she wore a drab brown skirt and sweater and a frayed white apron.

Near her stood a woman Art judged to be in her thirties,

22

tall and straight, in a dark green gown, red hair swept back from her face and bound in a single thick braid.

An immense black man in a brightly colored shirt and faded jeans stood beside the woman in green.

A short, swarthy woman with curly black hair could have passed for a gypsy fortune-teller; she wore a white blouse and leather slacks, though, rather than the traditional long skirt. Art wondered why on earth anyone would wear leather in August.

A middle-aged black woman in faded jeans and a floral-print blouse knotted at her midriff stood with her hands on her hips, arguing amiably with a rather smug-looking, mustached man in black slacks and a Hawaiian shirt.

An obese Oriental wearing only a pair of brown shorts stood panting in center stage, looking up at the flies.

Two swarthy men, one in a turban, were talking together well upstage, where Art couldn't see them clearly.

And a woman, or maybe only a girl, with light brown hair and a summer dress, sat on the edge of the stage, smiling at him.

They were an even more motley crew than most theater troupes, Art thought. He also wondered whether this was the entire company; Bampton Summer Theatre usually had twice this number.

But then, Bampton Summer Theatre was purely amateur.

Most of the others had turned when Ms. Fox leaped up on the stage, looking to see what the commotion was about. What desultory conversation they had been pursuing now died away completely as the entire company turned to stare at Art.

"Hi," he said, standing in the aisle feeling foolish.

Behind him, Innisfree cleared his throat.

"My fellow . . . ah, thespians!" Innisfree announced. "This is Arthur Dunham, our landlord's son. We are to make him welcome, as a requirement of our rental here!"

Most of the smiles that had been present had vanished.

"You think he's no trouble, Merle?" the black woman asked.

"Ah, my dear Tituba, trouble or no, what choice have we?" Innisfree called back.

"I won't be any trouble," Art said, annoyed. "I've worked here for years, done more than a dozen shows. I know where everything is, how everything works."

"You do not know how *we* work," the man with the mustache retorted. Art shrugged. "I'll learn. And I'll stay out of your way, if that's what you want."

"That is indeed what we want," the big black man replied. "We mean you no ill, Mr. Dunham, but we have our own ways."

"Well, that's fine, then," Art said, trying to hide his annoyance. "But my dad wants me here to keep an eye on the place, and Mr. Innisfree agreed, so here I am. Now, is there anything I can help with? Anything I can tell you about? Maybe show you somewhere you can put those things?" He pointed out the Duke of Athens's stage and the fairy queen's bower.

Several of the Bringers of Wonder turned to look where he pointed, as if noticing the retired sets for the first time.

"Can we use those?" the woman in green asked, directing her question not to Art, but to Innisfree.

"We don't need them," the black woman replied.

Innisfree turned up empty hands. "If you like, Faye, I'm sure we can find a use for them."

"Everyone already saw them in *Midsummer Night's Dream*," Art pointed out.

"Then we'll transform them," the woman in green said, "and none shall recognize them."

"Suit yourselves," Art said. "But if you'd rather just get rid of them, there's storage space in the basement, and there's a trapdoor upstage there that we can lower them down through—it'll take about five men, I'd say, two up here and three downstairs."

"Boy," the old woman in the kerchief snapped, startling Art, "haven't we told you to mind your own business? If we want 'em stashed, we'll do it ourselves!'' Her voice was no weak old woman's quaver, but sharp and strong; it cut through the theater like an oar through water.

That was *one* person who would have no trouble projecting to the back of the theater, Art thought. ''I'm sorry, Ma'am,'' he said, ''but it *is* my business—anything to do with this theater is.''

''Merle,'' the old woman said, glowering at Innisfree, ''if I'd known this place came with its own built-in twerp, I'd never have agreed to it.''

''Peace, Grandmother,'' said the man with the turban. ''Where *else* would we go?''

''Any number of places, you little snot,'' the old woman retorted. ''To Hell, for all of me. I didn't say I'd have gone elsewhere—I might just have gone home and said I'd have none of this whole lunatic production.''

''Oh, no,'' said the woman in green, ''you don't mean that! We *need* you!''

''She's right,'' the turbaned man agreed. ''We can't do it without you, Grandmother!''

''Listen,'' Art said, ''I'm sorry; I don't want to cause any trouble. I can just sit here and mind my own business, if that's really what you want.'' He stepped into a row of seats.

''I don't want you *anywhere*, nitwit,'' the old woman answered. ''I don't need some punk watching me.''

The others were uncomfortably silent for a moment; at last Innisfree suggested, ''I think that Ms. Yeager means we'd prefer to have no audience until we've got a little farther along.''

''All right,'' Art said. ''Then I'll go work on cleaning the basement. If you need anything, just come on down.''

He marched down the aisle, hopped one-handed up onstage—if Innisfree could do it, so could he—and found his way through the players to the stairway door in the stage-right wings.

The Bringers of Wonder watched him pass; then the woman who had been sitting on the stage got to her feet and called, "Hang on a minute, I'll come with you. I'd like to see what's down there."

He turned and smiled at her.

"Thanks," he said, "I'd be glad of the company."

Chapter Four

"MY NAME's Maggie," she said as they descended the narrow steps, "Maggie Gowdie."

"Art Dunham," Art said, reaching for the string that would turn on the dangling bare light bulb at the foot of the stair.

"Pleased to meet you. It's a long way down, isn't it?"

"Yes, it is. Watch your step." He stepped off the bottom stair onto the rough stone of the floor and turned to offer Maggie a hand. She accepted it and stepped down beside him, then looked around.

They were in a small room, perhaps eight feet square, with brown plank walls and a single door. Art pulled the key ring from his pocket, found the one he wanted, and unlocked the door; he opened it, reached inside, and flipped the light switch.

"Come on," he said.

Maggie followed him through the door into the basement's central corridor. Three lights in wire cages lit the ancient plaster walls of the narrow passage, walls that had been painted white once, long ago, but were now covered with scrapes, stains, and graffiti. At the near end the passage ended in a sliding door; at the other it turned a right angle into darkness. Closed doors were spaced along either side. The floor was raw granite; the foundations had been cut into the living bedrock. The ceiling, too, was stone, which startled Maggie. It was also some fifteen feet up.

"What a strange place!" she said.

"Yup," Art agreed. "Come on, we'll start at this end." He turned toward the sliding door, and Maggie followed.

"This seems like a lot of basement for a little old theater," she said, as he rolled the door aside. "And it looks different, too. I mean, upstairs is all wood, and down here there's stone."

"That's because the foundation's a lot older than the rest," Art explained. "Originally this place was a church, but it burned down. The crypts weren't damaged much, but everything else was a total loss. That was about 1910; it was a ruin until 1923, when someone bought it and built the theater."

Maggie looked over Art's shoulder into the gloom of the large room below the stage; he could smell the sweet odor of her hair. Light spilled in from the corridor and seeped, here and there, through cracks and knotholes in the floor overhead; there was no ceiling to hide the joists. They could hear voices—not well enough to make out words or even tell who was speaking, but enough to know when someone was talking. The air of the room had a cool, earthen feel, and Maggie could smell dry dust and moist soil.

Then Art flipped the light switch, and half a dozen wall fixtures came on, illuminating a strange and cavernous chamber.

Where visible, three of the walls were rough-hewn stone, while the floors above and below were simple plank—a sort of reversal of the corridor. When Maggie leaned forward to peer in she could see that the wall with the door in it was plaster, like the corridor. The wooden floor was a step down from the solid bedrock of the passage, which seemed completely unreasonable—why would anyone have cut farther down into the stone to make room for flooring?

Whatever the reason, they had done exactly that. Maggie continued her examination.

Stone columns were spaced along the three stone walls, curving over at the top as if to support a vaulted ceiling, but then ending in broken stumps. The stage floor above them rested on huge wooden beams, not on stone.

Between two of the columns, off to the right and well above the floor, was a huge double door to the outside, perhaps four yards square, held shut with a heavy wooden bar that rested in black iron brackets. A chain and padlock held the brackets closed and kept the bar in place.

Most of the wall space, and in fact almost half the total floor area, was filled with pieces of old sets—staircases and window seats, balconies and pulpits, all packed in together however they would fit. The dark greens of haunted forests shaded the vivid pinks and purples of nightclub stages, while staid floral wallpaper showed through Gothic arches. In the center of the chamber was a scattering of debris—Titania's wrap, Bottom's mask, Moon's lantern and thornbush—from the most recent production; cleaning that up was Art's major excuse for coming down here.

"This part was built about 1850," he said. "This end of the church fell in during the fire, which is why there's no ceiling. It's handy for the traps." He pointed to three trapdoors in the stage. Then he indicated the big door in the right-hand wall. "That's where we bring in lumber and so forth—it opens on a ramp up to the parking lot." He dropped his hand and pointed to the floor. "And there's another level underneath here, but we closed that off when I was a little kid—a lot of trash fell down there during the fire, or got thrown down there when the place was abandoned, and it wasn't much more than a stone pit to begin with, so when the old floor rotted we didn't replace the ladder or the door, we just put the new floor in over it."

"Your family's owned this place a long time, then?" Maggie asked.

"Oh, yes," Art agreed. "My grandfather bought it back

in the forties, during the postwar housing shortage. He wanted to convert it to a house and sell it, but he couldn't raise the capital.''

"So he left it a theater.''

"Right.'' Art cleared his throat. "Anyway, you're welcome to use any of these old sets, if you like. And you can store stuff down here. It's a little musty at this end— might have something to do with the pit, I suppose—but then there are plenty of storerooms under the house. The people who built the theater put walls in under each of the main support arches, and then ran that corridor down the center, so there are nine separate rooms, not counting the one with the stairs.''

Maggie nodded.

"And down the far end, around the corner, is where the water main and the electricity and phone lines come in.'' He pointed back down the corridor. "There's a small fuse box, too, for the outside lights. The main fuse box is upstairs near the lightboard, though.''

"Makes sense,'' Maggie said.

"Um,'' Art said, flicking off the lights in the big room, "is there anything else you'd like me to show you?''

"Well . . . what's in all the storerooms?''

"Mostly costumes on this side,'' he said, pointing, "and props on the other. And smaller set pieces; it's only the big ones we leave in there.'' He jerked a thumb toward the chamber beneath the stage, and as he did he caught, from the corner of his eye, a vivid blue flash, shining for an instant through the tiny openings in the floor above.

"What the hell . . .'' he said, angrily. "What are they doing up there?'' He turned and charged toward the stairs, forgetting Maggie.

She followed, calling after him, "Art, it's okay! Don't worry!''

He ignored her, rushing up the stairs at full speed and out through the open door into the backstage area.

"All right,'' he shouted, "who did that?''

The Bringers of Wonder all turned, startled, to face him.

"Did what?" Innisfree asked.

"I don't know," he said. "But I saw blue light, a bright flash of blue light—was one of you trying out the lighting instruments?"

Some of them shook their heads; a couple muttered, "No." The black woman—Tituba, Innisfree had called her—pointed at the shelves of equipment. "You mean those? Nobody touched those, boy."

Art could see the lights looked undisturbed; the main power switch for the lightboard was still off, the pilot light dark.

"Then what was it, a flashpot or something? Damn it, if you're going to be using pyrotechnics, let me know, so I can check 'em out and make sure we've got sand buckets ready!"

"No one used any fireworks, Mr. Dunham," the woman in green said.

Maggie had come up behind him. "Art," she said quietly, "I think it was just a camera flash."

Art turned to look at her, then turned back to find Innisfree holding up a camera.

"Maggie's right, Arthur," he said. "Just snapping a few 'before' shots for a little before-and-after."

Art hesitated.

"How'd you see it in the first place?" the old woman in the kerchief demanded.

"The cracks in the flooring," Art explained, pointing. After a moment's consideration, he said, "It seemed awfully bright for a camera flash."

"A trick of the eye, perhaps," Innisfree suggested.

"I guess so," Art agreed.

"Young man," the woman with the gypsyish looks said, "are you going to be rushing in here and interrupting us every time there's any little disturbance? Because if you are, that could be a serious problem."

"You know that our show involves magic, don't you?" the woman in green said. "We'll have things appearing and disappearing and flying about fairly often. And I wouldn't be surprised by a few flashes and bangs."

"Um," Art said thoughtfully.

"It *would* be inconvenient," Innisfree said.

"Sorry," Art said. He chewed his lower lip as he looked the lot of them over, then said, "Okay, but listen, *tell* me before you set off any fireworks, okay? And whoever's going to do lights, talk to me first, and let me help you set up."

"Assuredly," Innisfree said. "Certainly, by all means, and most assuredly!" He smiled ingratiatingly.

Uneasy but outnumbered, Art backed down from any further argument. In fact, it seemed like a wise idea to leave completely for a little while. "All right, then," he said. "I guess the basement can wait, anyway; I'll go take a little walk and leave you folks in peace for a bit."

"Our blessings upon you, then," Innisfree said, bowing.

Reluctantly, Art turned and walked out the stage door, uncomfortably aware of a dozen pairs of eyes watching him every step of the way.

Outside, the sun was painfully bright; he blinked, and shaded his eyes with his arm as he stood on the little porch, waiting for his pupils to adjust.

Spread out before him was the theater's little parking lot, only about a dozen spaces—for successful performances, the patrons lined the streets for blocks and usurped the parking lot of the bank across the street. The asphalt was bare and gray, baking in the August sun; a thin sifting of sand had found its way onto one corner.

The lot was empty.

His eyes had adjusted, but Art blinked again anyway.

There were no cars.

He looked out at the street, and saw no cars parked along the curbs. He scratched his head, baffled.

How the hell had the Bringers of Wonder *got* there? There were no hotels within what he'd have considered reasonable walking distance, and a motley bunch like that would have stood out on the Bampton streets on a Monday morning like seals in a schoolroom.

31

Someone must have given them a lift, he realized. Maybe there was another member of the group he hadn't met yet who was off buying supplies somewhere.

They'd have needed a bus, but they might very well *have* a bus, for all he knew.

And it didn't matter anyway. It was none of his business. As long as they didn't burn the theater down, they could arrive by dogsled for all he cared. With a shrug, he descended the four wooden steps and went for a stroll.

He didn't bother to knock when he came back from his walk; he just slipped quietly in through the stage door, trying not to disturb anybody.

The Bringers of Wonder were still sitting or standing about, talking quietly or looking over the theater. They had spread out somewhat—before, all but Innisfree had been onstage, but now the man with the turban was studying the lighting equipment—and not, Art was relieved to see, touching any of it—while Tituba and the woman in green looked over the ropes and ladders, the two Orientals studied the leftover sets, and two of the men, the big black one and the short one with the mustache, sat out in the middle of the house, chatting quietly. Innisfree was up in the balcony, poking through the dusty junk up there.

The rest were sitting either on the edge of the stage or in the front row, talking.

There were no signs that anything had been done toward organizing a performance; nobody was pacing out blocking, no scripts were in evidence, no one was giving direction.

Maggie, seated on the edge of the stage, turned at the sound of the door. She hopped up to her feet and crossed toward him, as several of the others cast unfriendly glares in his direction. Innisfree took a quick look, then turned and disappeared into the shadows farther up the balcony's slope.

"How's it going?" Art asked Maggie as she approached.

"Oh, fine," she said. "How was your walk?"

"Fine."

"We're almost done for today, I think."

"But it isn't even noon!" Art protested, startled.

"Oh, well, today was just sort of preliminary," Maggie said, with an offhand gesture. "You know, make sure everyone knew where the theater was, make sure we all knew each other, and so on. We can't really start on anything until the moon . . . I mean, until tomorrow night."

Tituba and the other—Faye, had someone called her?—moved away a little as Art and Maggie walked downstage.

"Make sure you all knew each other? I thought you folks had been together for a while," Art said.

Maggie shook her head. "Not really. We all knew *of* each other, I guess, but . . . well, Ms. Morgan wasn't on speaking terms with some of the others for the longest time, and Merle's been away, and I'm sort of filling in for my grandmother, I'm not . . . I haven't been around as long as the others."

Art nodded. "How'd you people get together, then?"

"That's hard to explain," Maggie said. "Family connections, you might say."

"Sure." Art stopped walking. "So today was just introductions? That's why there aren't any scripts or anything?"

"That's right."

"Are all the parts cast, though?"

Maggie hesitated. "I *think* so," she said.

"So who do you play?"

"Oh, I'm just in the chorus, really."

"What's the play again?"

"*The Return of Magic.* And it's not exactly a play, it's . . . it's a performance."

Art nodded. "Hope it goes over. Bampton's kind of old-fashioned; about as experimental as anyone's ever gotten around here was when they tried putting on Shaw's *Man and Superman*. And that was a disaster—must've been less than a third of the audience that stuck it out to the end."

"Oh, we're not worried."

"Well, that's good, I guess." He looked around, and then added, "Guess I'll go clear out that stuff downstairs. When you folks are ready to leave, let me know, and I'll lock up."

"All right." She smiled at him, then took his hand for a moment, gave it a quick squeeze, and turned away.

He watched her cross back to the edge of the stage; then he marched over to the stairway and down into the crypts.

Chapter Five

"ART?"

At the call Art looked up from the pile of dust and wood shavings that he'd swept together. The wrap and mask and lantern and the rest were all safely stashed away in the appropriate storerooms, which just left sweeping up.

"Art, we're going now; you can lock up any time." It was Maggie's voice coming from the stairwell.

"Thanks," he called back. He leaned the broom against the wall, fished the key ring from his pocket, and headed for the steps.

After he'd locked the door at the foot of the stairs he found that Maggie was waiting for him on the second landing.

"Mr. Innisfree said to tell you we'd need to be in by noon tomorrow, but we won't be doing any more mornings," she told him as he climbed the steps toward her.

"That's fine," he said. "I never heard of anyone doing theater work in the morning anyway."

"Well, I haven't done much theater," Maggie said. "I don't think any of us have, really, except maybe Ap . . . Mr. Tanner."

He reached her level, and the two of them proceeded up the narrow steps with her in the lead. "Why are you all doing it now, then?" he asked.

"Oh, well, *The Return of Magic* is special, and when Mr. Innisfree offered us a chance at it . . ." She shrugged.

"It's special?" Art asked. "I never heard of it."

"Hardly anyone has," Maggie agreed. "That's one reason it's special."

They reached the door at the top of the stairs and emerged backstage.

"Well, if it's like that," Art asked, "how'd you people hear of it, then?"

"Well, we're all interested in . . . well, magic," Maggie explained.

"Stage magic, you mean."

She smiled crookedly. "Yes, of course, stage magic."

"*That* explains things," Art remarked. "You mentioned magic before, too; I should have realized. No offense, but you folks don't look or act much like any other theater people I've worked with—but magicians, yeah, I can see that." He closed and locked the stairway door, after making sure the lights were all out.

He looked around and found the stage and wings empty.

"The others have gone already," Maggie explained.

Art nodded. "If you want to go on, I can finish up myself."

"No, that's all right, I'm not in any hurry."

"Okay, then, next stop is the lobby." He led her around by the stage-right steps, rather than jumping over the edge, and made his way up the aisle.

Maggie followed.

"So, you said your grandmother got you into this?" he asked, just to make conversation.

"That's right."

"She was a magician?"

"She was . . . well, she liked to claim she was a witch."

Art snorted. "She work up in Salem, for the tourists, or something?"

"No, no. Scotland."

Art turned, startled. "You're Scottish?"

"Grandmother was. I was born in Halifax."

"Oh. You don't have any accent."

Maggie grinned. "That's not what Grandmother's people said; they always told me I had the most awful American accent they'd ever heard."

"Well, that's what I meant, you don't have a Scottish accent."

"I grew up in . . . well, all over North America, really. My folks moved around a lot."

Art was silent for a moment before replying. "I think I might be jealous of all that moving," he said at last. "I've spent my whole life in Bampton. But I'm not *sure* I'm jealous, really; I like knowing where home is."

Maggie grimaced. "I know what you mean, and I don't think you should be jealous at all; I've never been sure where I belong. If anywhere. It's not a good feeling."

They had, by this time, emerged into the lobby; Art locked the doors, and for good measure threw the deadbolts. He was still upset that the Bringers of Wonder had found the place unlocked.

Then it was back across the lobby and down the aisle.

"So was it Innisfree who got all of you together and came up with the idea of staging *Return of Magic*?" Art asked, as much to make conversation as to get an answer. He found Maggie easy to talk to, and wanted to keep it that way, not let an awkward silence develop.

"Well, sort of," Maggie said. "I mean, the Bringers of Wonder, the group, was originally formed, oh, maybe seventy or eighty years ago, when M . . . when Mr. Innisfree wasn't around. And they always intended to do this—a production of *The Return of Magic*, I mean—but it wasn't until Mr. Innisfree turned up that they actually thought they might pull it off. They'd sort of let the group fall apart, but when he turned up everybody got back together. Except that I'm here instead of Grandmother, of course."

"Is Innisfree the director, then?"

Maggie hesitated slightly before answering. "Yes."

"So this play, *Return of Magic*—who wrote it?"

Again, she hesitated.

"I'm not really sure," she said at last. "You'll have to ask Mr. Innisfree."

Art nodded as he let her go up the steps to the stage ahead of him. He figured he could look it up at the library.

They were almost to the stage door when Maggie asked, "You said we weren't like theater people. What did you mean?"

Startled, Art glanced at her, then reached for the doorknob. "I mean you aren't," he said.

"How?"

"It's hard to explain, if you've never worked in the theater," Art said, opening the door. "There's a sort of . . . a sort of fellowship in the theater that you people don't seem to have. I mean, actors bicker with each other, and compete for parts, and try to upstage each other, but they always know they're all really on the same side, that they need each other."

"We know we need each other," Maggie protested, stepping out into the sun.

"But you don't know you need *me*," Art said, following her. "I'm theater, too, and you people just about threw me out of here."

"Well, we aren't used to having strangers watch us while we prepare," Maggie explained.

"But you *should* be," Art replied. "Actors love an audience, any time, any place, practically."

"Oh, I don't know," Maggie said. "I'd always heard that stars get tired of fans and spend half their time trying to get away from the public."

"That's not the same thing. Besides, you people aren't movie stars."

"You're just angry because you feel we've shut you out."

"No, I'm not," Art said, locking the door behind them and carefully keeping out of his voice anything that could be taken as a sign of resentment. "I don't care if you do, honestly; I was just surprised, because it's not like any theater people I ever saw before. But if you're magicians, that explains it—magicians have trade secrets to protect." He looked around.

"Hey, Art!" someone called.

He turned, and spotted Marilyn on the sidewalk. He waved.

He turned back, and Maggie was gone. Startled, he looked around, but didn't find her, or any of the other Bringers of Wonder.

She must have run down the steps and around the corner while he was locking the door, he decided—while he was still talking.

That was pretty rude—just the sort of thing he'd been trying to explain to her.

He shrugged and checked the door again, then thumped down the steps and shouted, "Hi, Marilyn!"

They ate lunch at Arby's, on the town square. Marilyn restricted herself to small talk until the sandwiches had been eaten; Art, certain she was dying to know who had rented the theater, admired her self-restraint.

When the last bite was in Art's mouth, though, Marilyn could restrain herself no longer.

"So what were you doing at the theater?" she asked.

"Just keeping an eye on things," Art replied, watching her closely.

"Oh." Marilyn was plainly disappointed. "So nobody's renting it after all?"

"What made you think someone might be renting it?" Art asked blandly.

"Oh, you know, I just . . . well, you were there this

morning, and someone said he saw your dad there yesterday. Nothing, really, I guess; I was just hoping.'' She
fluttered her hands in confusion.

Art decided it would be cruel to tease her any longer.
"Well, you're right," he said, "someone *did* rent it. They
were there this morning, making plans."

"Oh?" Her face lit up. "Who is it? What are they doing? I mean, is it a play, or just lectures, or something?"

"It's a play . . ." Art began.

"It is? What kind? Musical? Shakespeare?" Marilyn
was practically bouncing in her seat.

Art held up a restraining hand. "Whoa!" he said. "Let
me tell you!"

Marilyn grinned, and held a finger in front of her mouth.
"My lips are sealed," she said. "Death before further
interruption, I swear by the seven sacred soothsayers of
Samarkand. Speak, O font of all wisdom!"

"The seven sacred soothsayers of Samarkand?" Art
asked, grinning back.

Marilyn stared at him, but didn't say a word.

"Well, that's better, I guess," Art said, "whoever they
are."

She still held her mouth tightly closed as she bobbed
her head, and made beckoning gestures; Art had to fight
down laughter to continue.

"It's not anybody local," he said. "It's some group
called the Bringers of Wonder—I didn't get the details, but
apparently they travel around, and have been in business
for a long time, though they haven't been very active
lately."

Marilyn nodded, eyes wide.

"They're all magicians, and the show they're doing is
something called *The Return of Magic*, so I guess it's some
kind of magic show, more than a regular play."

"Oh, neat!" Marilyn said, oaths sworn by nonexistent
seers instantly forgotten. "You mean sort of like those
jugglers doing Shakespeare?"

"The Flying Karamazov Brothers. Yeah, maybe—I don't really know."

"So will they be holding auditions or anything?"

Art shook his head. "Nope. No local people at all, not in the show, not even backstage—at least, that's what they've said so far. I'm only there because my dad insisted—I'm his agent and fire marshal, more than their crew. I guess I'll be helping with the lights, but that's . . . well, they don't like outsiders."

Marilyn blinked in surprise. "They don't?" she said. "You mean not even theater people?"

"Not even theater people," Art confirmed. "Remember, they're magicians—they're kind of paranoid, I guess about people learning secrets about their tricks."

"That's *silly*," Marilyn said.

Art shrugged. "I won't argue," he said.

"So I can't work on the show?"

"Probably not." Art hesitated, and then said, "Look, if there's any chance at all, I'll try to get you in, but I can't promise anything. They're pretty strange."

"Really?" Marilyn set her elbows on the table, laced her fingers together, and leaned forward, resting her chin on the back of her hands. "Tell me more!"

Chapter Six

ART SWUNG open the stage door and stepped into the dim, dry heat of the theater. He slid the key ring into his pocket and found the switch for the backstage work lights.

The lights came on, faint and yellow after the blaze of the summer sun out in the parking lot, and he closed the door behind him.

The inside of the empty theater smelled of dust and old wood and ancient paint, of yellowed paper and crumbling fabric—an attic smell, a hot summer smell that Art found wonderfully comforting. Nothing was disturbed here, nothing was dangerous; everything was safely dead and desiccated, dried out and folded up and put away, tucked away in neat jumbles of mystery, in trunks and boxes, on shelves and in stacks, to be taken out only as needed. The storerooms were packed with wonders and marvels, all of them safely false, just sequins and tissue paper, papier-mâché and poster paint.

Beyond the open curtain the house was dark; the even rows of empty seats were parallel lines of deepening blackness, stretching to an apparent infinity—but really only to the invisible and reassuring rear wall.

There were times when Art admitted to himself that he liked the theater best when it was empty and dark like this, no one here but himself, with all its hidden treasures his own, all its store of imagination unshared, no one imposing a playwright's dreams on him. It was his own personal playhouse, in every sense of the word.

He strolled downstage, into the dimness, his footsteps loud on the wood; outside he could hear the distant buzzing of summer—lawn mowers and insects and traffic, all of it diminished by distance. The heat in the theater was stifling, his shirt prickled with sweat, but just now he didn't care. The theater had air conditioning—the switches were in the lobby, near the box office—but of course, he hadn't left it turned on overnight.

He would turn it on in a moment, but for now he wanted to just sit and think a little.

The Bringers of Wonder were due any minute; Art supposed they would start blocking out their show. Had they already assigned roles, decided who would provide costumes and props and so forth?

Well, that wasn't his concern, was it? He was here if they needed him—just as he was in his winter job, driving a snowplow for the town. Most of the time, all he had to do was be somewhere they could reach him, and for that they paid him ten dollars a day; when the snow started falling, he worked, and they paid him ten dollars an hour. Bampton wasn't big enough or rich enough to hire full-time snowplow drivers.

When he worked depended on the whims of the weather; in a mild winter he didn't have much to do, while in a bad one he worked almost constantly. He was accustomed to that.

His summer work had always been different, though; Bampton Summer Theatre had always kept to a schedule, kept him busy for exactly so many evenings. There had always been plenty to do—even when everything was designed and hung and wired and gelled and focused and tested, he could find ways to tinker, to fine-tune the lights, and there was always cleaning to be done.

And if he had nothing important to do, he could watch the rehearsals and offer advice.

The Bringers, it seemed, were going to be different.

He sat down on the edge of the stage and looked out at the darkened seats, his eyes steadily adjusting. He wondered whether it would have been a good idea to bring a book to read; if the Bringers weren't going to keep him busy, he'd need something to do. Especially if they didn't want him watching.

It wouldn't be practical to build the strip lights he wanted; first, because he didn't have the money for materials, and second, because he couldn't use the stage to work on while the Bringers were there.

Well, the basement wasn't as clean and tidy yet as it could be; this was a chance to tackle long-neglected corners in the storerooms down there, maybe clear out old junk that no one was ever going to use again.

All the same, bringing a book might have been clever. He would plan on dropping by the library tomorrow morning and finding something good. Someone had mentioned a couple of possibilities—had that been Jamie, during rehearsals for *Midsummer Night's Dream*? Or George?

"Ah, Arthur," Innisfree's voice said. "A pleasure to see you."

Art started, and looked over his shoulder.

The Bringers were on the stage behind him—not just Innisfree, but several of them, perhaps all of them.

Art scooted himself off the stage and turned to face them. "I didn't hear you come in," he said.

"Well, we didn't want to disturb you," Innisfree explained. "You looked so thoughtful, sitting there."

Art had not realized he was being particularly thoughtful, and did not understand how he had failed to hear the stage door opening and closing, had failed to hear footsteps on the stage, had failed to see the sunlight when the door was opened. He made no answer, but instead simply stood, looking up at Innisfree, and the old woman, and the woman with the braid—she wasn't in green today, but in a gown of maroon silk that looked totally inappropriate for such hot weather.

"What the devil are you staring at, boy?" the old woman shouted. Her voice was *incredibly* piercing.

"Nothing," Art said. "You startled me, ma'am, that's all." She was, he noticed, wearing either the same clothes as yesterday, or others equally dismal and unmemorable. Like the other woman's, they were far heavier than was reasonable on a hot August day.

"That's no reason to stare like a damned owl."

"Sorry." Art blinked and turned his gaze elsewhere.

Maggie was off to stage right, watching him; she wore cutoff jeans and a red paisley halter.

"Well," Innisfree called, "I think we're all here; shall we get started?"

"What, you expect us to get anything done with this idiot staring at us as if we were his television set?" the old woman demanded. "It's pretty clear he doesn't have the wit for anything more complicated than TV."

"Baba," Innisfree said, "leave the boy alone. You know why he's here."

"All the same, sir," said the man with the elegant mus-

tache, "I think we would all be happier if he did not remain where he is, watching us from the audience."

Innisfree looked about, confounded, as a general round
of nodding and affirmative muttering greeted this.

"It's all right," Art said, coming to Innisfree's rescue,
"I've still got some things I can do down in the basement.
If you need anything, you can send someone down, or just
call through one of the traps."

Innisfree's relief was obvious. "Thank you, Arthur,
you're a gentleman."

"You're welcome," Art said, as he headed for the steps
up to the stage.

Maggie met him there, and walked beside him to the
basement door; she glanced back over her shoulder, then
whispered, "Don't mind Ba . . . I mean, Ms. Yeager.
She's just as disagreeable with everyone."

"Yeager?" Art threw the old woman a quick glance,
which she nonetheless seemed to catch. When he turned
away again he was sure she was glaring at him.

Maggie nodded. "Barbara Yeager. Her friends call her
Baba—if she has any friends."

Art paused with his hand on the doorknob and looked
at Maggie, noticing the sweat on her forehead. He still
hadn't turned on the air conditioning, and the stage was
hot.

"I'd sort of like to know who everybody is," he said.
"Nobody's ever done any real introductions, and I don't
like not even knowing any names."

Maggie blinked. "Well, you know *my* name."

"That's true," Art admitted. "And I know Mr. Innisfree, but you people call him something else."

"Oh—Merle, I guess you mean. That's his first name.
M-E-R-L-E, like Merle Haggard."

Art nodded. "And the Chinese woman's name is Fox?
Like the animal?"

Maggie nodded. "I don't know her first name," she
said, apologetically.

"Are you two going to stand there jabbering all day?" the old woman demanded.

"Just a minute, Grandmother!" Maggie called back.

"Is she your grandmother, the one who said she was a witch?" Art asked, whispering.

"Oh, no, of course not!" Maggie stifled a laugh. "No, we just call her that. I think she likes it. She's Russian, you know, and 'Baba' is short for 'Barbara,' but it's also the Russian word for 'Granny,' so . . . well, anyway, I don't think she really has any kids or grandkids of her own, and none of us are directly related. Except maybe Merle and Faye. I think they're connected somehow, cousins or something."

"Who's Faye?"

"Faye Morgan, the redhead with the braid." She pointed.

Art glanced at the woman in maroon silk. Yes, he'd heard her called Faye; it had slipped his mind. "What about . . ." he began.

"Maggie!" the redhead called. "Could you come here?"

"Go ahead," Art said, opening the door. "Thanks."

Maggie turned to see what Faye Morgan wanted, and Art switched on a light and descended into the relative coolness of the basement.

He wondered how long it would be before someone asked him how to turn on the air conditioning; he had intended to do that, but had gotten distracted.

For the present, he didn't worry about it—the basement was cool enough that he wouldn't suffer, and the Bringers, as they had made abundantly clear, weren't his problem. He found the dustpan and broom; the little heap of dust and wood shavings was just where he had left it, waiting to be cleared away.

He could hear footsteps overhead as the Bringers went about their business—whatever it was. His playhouse wasn't private anymore.

Down here, the theater's odor was just as distinctive,

but different—the hot attic smell of dry wood was thin and faint, almost lost in the cool dark cellar fragrance of earth and must and damp stone.

Cellars below, attic above, and nothing in between; the theater was treasure house and playroom, but no one's home.

He swept up the mound of debris and dumped it in the battered steel drum that served as a trashcan. That done, he returned broom and dustpan to their regular places, and then stood, eyes closed, in the center of the big room.

Below him, he knew, was the pit in the stone that he had told Maggie about; he remembered seeing it when he was just a kid, maybe four or five years old. It had been a dark square surrounded by gray stone that seemed to go down and down and down forever, deep into the secret black heart of the world; it had terrified and fascinated him. He remembered that he had thought it smelled strange, and a faint draft had seemed to blow down into it, as if something huge and moist and alien were down there, breathing slowly in, trying to suck him down into the blackness.

He supposed that whoever built the church had intended it as a crypt of some sort; it had been too big for a well. So far as he had ever heard, though, no one was entombed there; it was just a big square empty hole that later generations had dumped trash into.

He hadn't seen any trash as a kid, so far as he could recall, but all the grown-ups had told him it was down there.

Maybe they should have left it open, he thought, and gone on dumping trash down there until they filled it; it would have been easier than hauling the steel drum out through the big outside door every so often to empty it.

Now, though, with the new floor in place for eighteen years, there was no sign that the pit existed, or had ever existed. He couldn't feel any air moving through the cracks in the floor, couldn't smell that strange scent over the ordinary stone and moisture of the basement.

He opened his eyes and listened.

The Bringers were moving around overhead, going about their business—whatever it was. He could hear voices muttering, but could make out no words. He could hear footsteps as they moved about, but no pattern, no organization. No one was calling instructions, no one was moving sets.

He wondered just what sort of a show this *Return of Magic* really was; was it a play, or a magic act, or what?

Well, it apparently wasn't his business, and nobody was calling for him to come turn on the air conditioning, or to help hang lights, or to show them where anything was. Irritated, he turned and marched out into the passageway, where he pulled the key ring from his pocket and unlocked the first door on the right.

He turned on the light inside the door and looked at a long, tall, narrow room lined with shelves—to either side the shelves were built onto the wooden walls, while at the far end freestanding storage racks stood against the rough stone of the foundation. Most of the shelves were filled with cardboard boxes; a few held loose items, sometimes neatly stacked, sometimes shoved onto the shelves in heaps.

This room was dedicated to small props and set dressing—things like silverware and lampshades and vases. Sorting through all this would, he was sure, keep him busy for hours.

Maybe days.

An hour or so later he rolled the steel drum in from the big room; the objects deemed too far gone to be worth saving had overflowed the box he had chosen for their disposal, and he had barely started.

Chapter Seven

It still seemed as if he had scarcely begun when he heard Maggie's voice calling, "Art? Are you down here?"

He put down the chrome cocktail-ice mallet he had been studying and called in reply, "In here!"

A moment later the witch's granddaughter stuck her head through the doorway and smiled at him.

"Hi," she said. "We're all done for today."

Art glanced at his watch and read 5:44. "Dinner break?"

"No, we're finished for today."

"Okay." He looked over the various objects he had pulled out of the box he was working on, and shrugged. "I'll do the rest of this tomorrow, I guess."

"What are you doing?" Maggie asked, stepping into the room.

"Sorting," he said.

Maggie looked at the rows of boxes. Some were labeled, in a variety of different hands and using a variety of implements, from charcoaled stick to fountain pen to felt-tip marker, from crayon to pencil to paint; others were not marked in any way. Some of the inscriptions were cryptic—"E Laws 3rd C'nut," for example—while others, such as "Cocktail set, Christie's Mousetrap, 1973 production," were clear. Many boxes bore names, or dates, or descriptions of contents, or some combination thereof; most of the names were unfamiliar, and the dates went back at least as far as 1926.

"What *is* all this stuff?" Maggie asked.

"Props," Art told her. "If you need any for this show you're doing, let me know, and I'll see if I can find them for you."

"Where'd they all come from?"

Art shrugged. "They just sort of accumulated. People

48

would pick them up at yard sales for a show, or find them in attics, or make them"—he gestured at a foot-long prop dagger made of wood painted silver, the wood cracked with age and the paint flaking—"and then after the show, they'd just leave them here in case someone needed them again later."

Maggie nodded. "I think I see," she said slowly. "This explains a lot."

"It does?" Art looked around, puzzled; he didn't see how the prop room explained anything at all.

"Never mind that," Maggie said briskly, in an abrupt change of tenor. "I came down to tell you we're leaving, and we'll want to get back in tomorrow at two o'clock."

"Two?"

"Yup."

Art looked around.

This could wait, he decided. He would have plenty of time to get it done before the Bringers held their one and only performance on August 30th. He picked up the ice hammer, placed it atop the 1973 cocktail set box, then turned off the light and herded Maggie out the door before closing and locking it behind them.

At the top of the stairs, when they emerged into the backstage area, Art was startled to realize that the air was cool and sweet, the hot, dry, dusty air of the morning gone. The Bringers must have figured out for themselves how to turn the air conditioner on, he decided. He would need to check on that and make sure they had turned it off again.

The only illumination came from the backstage work lights; the stage was dim, the house dark, the lobby doors closed, so far as he could see. Maggie, paying no attention, headed for the stage door, while Art turned toward the steps.

"Where are you going?" Maggie asked, startled.

"Oh, I need to check the place over," Art said, "make sure you people left everything where it belongs. You go ahead, you don't have to wait for me."

Maggie hesitated, then answered, "All right," as Art descended the steps from the stage.

He waved a quick farewell; when he turned to say good-bye the stage door was closing behind her.

He hesitated, slightly irked at her quick exit—though he knew that was unreasonable of him. He'd said himself that she didn't have to wait. Then he shrugged off his annoyance and marched up the aisle to the lobby, through the lobby to the box office, and back to the control panel.

The air conditioner was off, the thermostat still set where he had left it; he put his hand on the air conditioner housing, and could feel no coolness. The metal was room temperature.

They must have turned it off a while ago, he decided. But usually the theater heated up fast. Had it cooled off outside? The weather reports hadn't predicted that.

Puzzled, he went on about his business, checking all the doors. When at last he emerged at the rear of the theater the sun was swimming on the horizon, bloated and red, and the air was still furnace-hot.

He stood on the back porch for a moment, trying to figure it out.

Then, with a shrug, he gave up and went home for dinner.

Chapter Eight

THE TOWN library's copy of the book Jamie had particularly recommended, Ray Bradbury's *Something Wicked This Way Comes*, was already checked out; Art checked the entire shelf twice, just to be sure.

He couldn't remember any other titles. He could have just chosen a book at random, but he hated doing that; he'd gotten too many boring volumes that way.

It was ten-thirty, and he didn't have to be anywhere until two—well, quarter of, to be safe—and he couldn't find the book he wanted.

Annoyed, he turned and saw the card catalog, and a thought struck him. He crossed to the wooden cabinet and found the title index, then looked under R.

Return of the King, *Return of the Native*—no, there wasn't any "the" in the middle. *Return of Nathan Brazil*, *Return of Monte Cristo*, *Return of Mr. Moto*, *Return of Martin Guerre*, *Return of Lysander* . . .

No *Return of Magic*.

He flipped a few dozen cards in either direction without finding it; then he tried under "The," just in case.

It wasn't there, either.

He gave up on the title index and tried by subject, under "drama," "magic," and "theater."

No luck.

Well, Bampton's library was pretty good for a small town, but it still didn't amount to much compared to a big-city library or a university's. They probably just didn't have the play in their collection.

But they might have a mention of it somewhere; he left the card catalog and found the theater section.

Most of the books were obviously not going to help much, but a few looked promising; he pulled them out and thumbed through the indices.

The Return of Magic was not a Restoration comedy, apparently; he found some impressive lists of those. It wasn't mentioned in books on medieval mummers' plays, passion plays, and the commedia dell'arte. It wasn't by Shakespeare or Shaw or Ibsen or Chekhov; it had never been a Broadway hit.

He frowned.

Maybe if he knew who wrote it—going through every single playwright's biography would take forever. And it might have an alternate title, for that matter.

He would have to ask about that.

It was almost noon by the time he abandoned the search,

and even if he hadn't found a book, he had at least managed to use up the morning; he went home for lunch, and then headed to the theater at about one-thirty, equipped with a couple of old magazines to read while waiting for the Bringers.

He had been sitting on the edge of the stage reading the June issue of *Esquire* for perhaps ten minutes when he heard footsteps behind him. He put the magazine down and turned, and found Innisfree standing at center stage, ludicrous in Bermuda shorts and a Hawaiian shirt.

Again, Art had not seen or heard anyone come in; he was beginning to find these silent entrances and exits rather aggravating.

"Hi, Mr. Innisfree," he said, putting down his magazine.

"Good afternoon, Arthur, and a fine day it is, too!"

Art had his own opinion on that, which was that it was still too damned hot out—he had turned the air conditioning on as soon as he could, and it was just now beginning to cut through the dry, dusty heat of the theater. He didn't say anything about that. Instead, he remarked, "I've been wondering—what's this play of yours about?"

Innisfree blinked at him. "What's that?" he asked.

"This play you're putting on, *The Return of Magic*—what's it about?"

Innisfree cleared his throat. "Well, that's a bit hard to say."

Art suppressed the urge to say, "Try." Instead he just looked up expectantly and waited.

"Well," Innisfree said, "you see, it's about a group of wizards and sorcerers who are worried about their magic fading away, and who gather together to seek out a new source of power."

"Sounds interesting," Art said. "Lots of special effects and fancy lighting, I suppose." He glanced at the shelves where the lighting instruments and cables remained untouched.

"Well, I suppose; we haven't got into that yet," Innisfree said uneasily.

"Could I see a script?" Art asked.

"I'm afraid we don't have any extra copies," Innisfree replied, apologetically. "In fact, some of us are sharing as it is."

"Well, I could make some photocopies if you want . . ."

"No, thank you—that might get us in trouble. The proprietors are very picky about that."

Art nodded. "Maybe I could find you some more, then," he suggested. "Who wrote it?"

Innisfree smiled crookedly. "No one you ever heard of, I'm afraid," he said. "And I doubt you'll find copies."

"I might," Art said. "You might be surprised what one can find here in Bampton. Who was it?"

Innisfree smiled. "A fellow named Merton Ambrose," he said. "Or at least, that's the name he used; I suspect it's a stage name."

Art nodded. "I'll take a look," he said.

"For what?" someone asked. Art started, and realized that the woman with the curly black hair was in the stage-right wings. He hadn't seen her come in. She was wearing a low-cut sundress and white sandals, and was walking toward them.

"For *The Return of Magic*," Art replied. "Mr. Innisfree said you could use another copy or two of the script."

"Oh, did he?" She gave Innisfree a look Art couldn't even begin to interpret, and stopped two paces away.

"Yes, Ms. . . . I'm sorry, I didn't get your name?"

The black-haired woman turned her inscrutable gaze on Art, then smiled wryly.

"My stage name," she said, "Is Kaye. Kier Kaye, K-I-E-R K-A-Y-E. I can't say I really care for it anymore, but I seem to be stuck with it."

"It's pretty," Art said, truthfully.

"Ha!" another voice interjected. "The lad thinks he knows beauty!"

Art looked, and discovered the mustached man off to

stage left, in embroidered white shirt and loose black pants.

"Arthur Dunham," Kier Kaye said, "allow me to introduce Dr. Eugenio Torralva, a man whose blessings sound like curses."

Dr. Torralva bowed deeply. "Your servant, sir," he said.

"Hello," Art replied.

Now, *these* two seemed like actors—the flamboyant bow, the snide remark, that was the sort of behavior he expected from theater people.

He discovered that while he had been speaking to this pair, the rest of the Bringers of Wonder had somehow arrived—though again, he hadn't seen or heard the stage door open. "Hello," he said again, this time directing it to the entire group.

Old Ms. Yeager glowered at him; Maggie smiled. One of the men gestured, and pulled a flame from thin air; it seemed to burn without fuel between his thumb and forefinger, a bright orange flame four or five inches high. Then he parted his fingers, and it was gone.

Art hesitated, unsure whether he should applaud, or whether the sudden sleight-of-hand demonstration had any purpose at all. And of course, playing with fire wasn't necessarily safe, in the dry old wooden building, and maybe, in his role as fire marshal, he should say something about it. "Uh . . ." he said, "Ms. Kaye, who is that?"

She smiled again.

"Apollonius!" she called. "Would you come here a moment?"

The man who had conjured the flame strode over to them. He was tall and rather thin, old enough that his hair was white, but he was still straight and strong, with few wrinkles; he wore a white robe that looked vaguely Arabic, and Art was unsure whether this was a costume or his normal street wear.

"Kier," he said.

"Your little stunt caught our young friend's eye," she told him. "Art, this is Apollonius . . . Apollonius Tanner."

"Call me Al," the tall man said, holding out a hand.

"Art," Art said, shaking.

Before he could say anything more, issue a warning about open flames, Yeager interrupted, calling, "Can we get on with this?"

"Yes," Innisfree immediately said, rubbing his hands together and marching to center stage. "I think we should get started."

"Then get that damned kid out of here!" Yeager demanded, pointing at Art.

The open flame wasn't worth arguing about.

"I'm going," Art said. He climbed up on the stage, tucked his magazines under his arm, and marched toward the basement stairs. Behind him, he heard a few murmurs uneasily raised in his defense; he ignored them.

After all, he had plenty of sorting still to go.

As he descended the steps he reviewed the names he had learned so far, and concluded that he could now attach a name to eight of the twelve Bringers; he still wasn't sure of either of the two blacks, or the fat Oriental guy, or the one in the turban, but he knew the others. And the black woman's name was Tituba, he thought.

In the storeroom he found the boxes and props as he had left them—but the gleam of metal caught his eye the instant he turned on the light.

He knelt and looked over the heap of unsorted objects, and saw what it was he had spotted. He pulled a foot-long dagger from the pile.

It was a fine piece of work, a glittering steel blade and a hilt of carved bone, colored dyes worked into the patterns on the grip. It looked archaic, ancient, really, but the metal shone like new.

He had never seen it before.

He was quite sure of that; he would have remembered a thing like that. It looked valuable, and out of place in the jumble of dusty, worthless props. How had he missed it yesterday?

He held it up, studying the play of light on the razor-sharp blade.

Nobody would use that thing onstage, he thought. Far too dangerous, with an edge like that; sooner or later someone would get cut, would wind up with bloody fingers or a slashed costume at the very least. So what was it doing here?

He looked down at the pile, puzzled.

Knives—where had he been putting prop knives?

Hadn't there been a wooden one, with peeling paint, in this pile? Had he put that somewhere?

It certainly wasn't here now.

He stared at the pile for a moment, then sighed, seated himself cross-legged on the floor, and placed the dagger carefully to one side.

That was an exotic, expensive-looking knife. Perhaps one of the Bringers of Wonder had lost it, and it had somehow wound up down here? Dropped through a trapdoor, perhaps?

No, the traps all came out in the big room, not the prop storeroom.

Maybe it had been caught in his clothes and then had fallen out down here? Or maybe that Apollonius guy was playing a little trick of some kind?

That reminded him that he had never issued a warning about conjuring up fire, the way Al, or Apollonius, or whatever his name was, had.

Well, it could wait. And he would figure out later where the knife came from. For now, he had sorting to do.

He ignored the dagger and began pulling items one by one from the pile.

Chapter Nine

THAT EVENING Maggie's call to lock up didn't come until seven. Art had lost track of time, and hadn't noticed his empty stomach. He hurried home, but was too late to join his father at the table; he had to scrounge up his own dinner.

He had intended to ask the Bringers if they could identify the mysterious bone-handled knife, but he had missed his chance; all but Maggie were long gone, and by the time he remembered his intention she, too, had left.

The next day's call was for four in the afternoon, Maggie told him; that meant he had plenty of time to go through the theater books in the Bampton library again, this time looking for any reference to Merton Ambrose.

He found not a trace; the name did not appear anywhere. Not in the card catalog, not in the theater books, not in any of the reference books he checked.

Frustrated, he wandered out onto the sidewalk, where he found Marilyn sitting on the ornamental stone wall by the Leader Federal Savings Bank. She waved at him.

He hesitated, then strolled down the block and hoisted himself up beside her.

For a moment the two of them sat side by side in friendly silence, enjoying the shade of the maples and studying the scattered spots of afternoon sunlight that had found a path through the leaves and now wandered about the sidewalk beneath their dangling feet.

It couldn't last forever, though. "Ever hear of Merton Ambrose?" he asked, still watching the play of light. A solitary ant was scouting the concrete, he noticed.

She considered the question carefully while she, too, watched the ant, and then looked up and replied, "No; should I have?"

Art shrugged.

"Is he an actor?" she asked. "TV, or movies?"

"No," Art told her, turning his attention from the ground to his companion's face. "He's a playwright. Or a magician, maybe. He wrote the play that those people are staging."

"Oh!" Marilyn was suddenly intensely interested; she forgot all about the ant and the sunlight and the maples. "Merton Ambrose, was it?"

Art nodded.

"And it's called *The Return of Magic*, you said?"

"Yup."

Marilyn glanced past Art at the library, and said, "I take it you were just looking it up; what's it about?"

"I didn't find it," he answered. "Didn't find a trace of it anywhere. It's gotta be really obscure."

Marilyn thought that over, then shrugged. "Well, at least it'll be different, then; I don't think I could stand seeing *Oklahoma!* one more time."

"I don't know," Art said, trying to spot the ant again. "There's something funny about the whole thing."

She blinked at him, then asked, "Why?"

"Oh, I don't know, a lot of little things." Art hesitated, and then explained, "They won't let me watch them rehearse—but they can't really be rehearsing yet, and why shouldn't I watch blocking? I haven't seen a script, or any costume sketches, or anything; they haven't touched the lights, or started building sets. And I haven't heard anyone say a *single line* from the show!"

"They won't let you watch?" Marilyn stared at him. "Then what have you been *doing* all day?"

He grimaced. "Cleaning the prop room—I've been meaning to do that for years, to go through all that junk down there and throw out most of it. Or maybe sell it, hold a big rummage sale."

"Good idea," she said, thoughtfully.

Art didn't bother to answer.

They sat silently for a moment, Art staring down at the cracks in the sidewalk, Marilyn watching him do it. The ant had gone.

Marilyn was the next to speak. "They haven't started on the sets or anything?" she asked.

"Nope."

"So what are *they* doing, while you're cleaning the prop room?"

Art shrugged. "I don't know. I honestly can't figure it out."

"Do you think they're really getting ready for a show? I mean, maybe it's one of these minimalist things, with a bare stage. Or they've got a set ready-built somewhere that's getting shipped in."

"Really, Marilyn, I just don't know," Art told her. "I don't have any idea at all."

"If they aren't doing a show," she persisted, "what *are* they doing?"

"Marilyn, I *don't know*," he insisted.

"Are they dealing drugs, maybe?"

Art shook his head. "Nobody else ever comes to the theater," he said. "Where are their customers?"

"If you're in the basement all day, how do you *know* nobody comes?"

Annoyed, Art found himself unable to answer that. A week ago he'd have said he could hear people come in, but after a couple of days with the Bringers, who almost seemed to appear out of thin air and then vanish just as mysteriously, he was no longer going to make any such claim.

Marilyn didn't press the point. Instead, she suggested, "Or maybe it's prostitution; didn't you say they were mostly women?"

"Not mostly," Art protested. "About half of them, same as any bunch of actors. It's just the ones who talk to me are the women."

Marilyn nodded.

Art added, "And that's normal enough, too, I guess."

"So maybe the men are pimps . . ."

Art sighed. "You're being silly," he said. "One of the women looks about ninety and talks like Don Rickles, and one of the others looks like, I dunno, Pearl Bailey or somebody. The others all look good enough, I guess, but what's that, four hookers to support a dozen people?''

"So maybe the men peddle their asses, too."

"In Bampton? Oh, come on!"

"Sure, in Bampton!"

"A bunch of strangers, coming to Bampton for that?"

It was Marilyn's turn to have no good answer; after a pause, she said, "Okay, so they're dealing drugs . . ."

Art turned away in disgust and slid down off the wall.

"Hey, wait, Art, I'm sorry!" Marilyn called.

Art stopped, and waited, standing by her knees. He didn't look at her; instead he studied the stones that had been fitted together to make the wall on which she sat— or perhaps had just been stuck on the surface, it was hard to be sure. In any case, the wall was hardly traditional New England dry stone; it was obviously held together with mortar or cement.

When she was certain that he wasn't about to depart, Marilyn asked, "Okay, so do you really think they're putting on this play?"

Art shrugged. "What else *could* they be doing?"

"Umm . . . kiddie porn, maybe? Or some kind of cult thing?"

At that Art looked up. There was that mysterious knife to explain—with its bone grip and strange carvings, might it be some sort of ritual dagger?

He didn't want to get Marilyn off on another tangent, though.

"Maybe," he said.

"If you figure it out, tell me," Marilyn said. "Or just give me a call sometime anyway."

"All right," he said.

For a moment the two of them remained as they were, looking at each other without making direct eye contact; then Art turned away.

"Guess I'll go sort some more old props," he said.

"Have fun," she said.

She sat on the wall, watching him go.

The dimness of the theater seemed somehow different today, Art thought; it wasn't as familiar and comforting. Maybe that was because, this late in the day, the theater was hotter than outdoors—it held the heat. He ambled up the aisle to the lobby and got the air conditioning running.

The Bringers weren't due for almost an hour. He wasn't exactly sure why he had come early; sorting props wasn't exactly his idea of a grand and glorious good time. Sitting in the shade talking to Marilyn *was* a good way to pass the time, but somehow he hadn't wanted to stay there.

There was something a little uncomfortable in his friendship with Marilyn just now; he figured it was because she was going to be leaving in a month. What was the point in getting closer to her when she would be leaving, and he would be staying?

Better to just keep his mind on his work, such as it was.

He took his time coming down the aisle again, and used that time to study the proscenium, the curtain, the stage.

It all looked just as it had three and a half days ago, when the Bringers had first arrived; they hadn't so much as moved the curtain, so far as he could tell. There were no sets, no props.

However, he realized, he did see marks on the stage—those would presumably be for blocking, for showing the cast who belonged where in various scenes. He climbed up on the stage and looked.

Every other production he'd ever worked on had used colored tape for blocking marks, but the Bringers had used chalk, white and red chalk. They had drawn a white circle center stage, about fifteen feet in diameter, with little red symbols here and there around the circumference.

It was a very neatly drawn circle, obviously not done freehand; the symbols, on the other hand, looked like little more than scribbles to Art. He could make no sense of any of them.

As he walked around the circle, he remembered Marilyn's suggestion that the alleged play was a cover for some sort of cult activity. The idea had a certain plausibility that made him uneasy; this chalk figure could be some sort of pentagram for an occult ritual.

But it was probably just blocking marks.

Maybe the play had some sort of ritual *in* it. It was about magic, after all.

But what if it *was* some kind of occult ceremony these people were planning, rather than a play? What then?

Well, *what* then? What business was it of his?

Not much. People had a right to their own beliefs. That was in the Constitution.

But it would mean they had lied to him, and to his father, and that was wrong, that was a violation of the rental contract. And why would they lie? It wasn't any big deal if they wanted to hold a ritual, was it?

And why in the theater? There were some local pagans in Bampton, people who called themselves Wiccans, who held meetings, and they always held them outdoors, not in theaters.

So the Bringers weren't Wiccans, obviously. Maybe they were Satanists, and the fact that the foundation had originally been a church had appealed to them.

But Maggie had apparently not known that the theater was built atop a ruined church until he had told her.

He looked down at the chalk lines on the scuffed wood of the stage and frowned. He was being silly. They were just a bunch of actors and prestidigitators. These were blocking marks. And the knife in the basement wasn't anything special; someone had dropped it somewhere, that was all, and it had wound up in the prop room by accident.

But why couldn't he find any mention of Merton Ambrose or *The Return of Magic*? It was all rather odd.

He would, he decided, bring the knife up here and wait for the Bringers, and ask a few questions. Simple enough.

When he started down the stairs the theater was empty and silent. By the time he had fetched the dagger and started back up, even though it was still ten minutes before four, he could hear voices; the Bringers had begun to arrive.

He was spotted the instant he reached the top of the stairs. "Ah, Arthur!" Innisfree called. "I'd wondered where you were!"

"I was getting this from the basement," Art explained, carefully holding the knife out by the blade, hilt extended. "I think one of you must have left it here the other day."

Innisfree and Morgan, the two closest of the four Bringers in sight, came to look.

"A fine weapon," Morgan said, "but not mine."

"Nor mine," Innisfree said. He looked up and gestured to the man in the turban—who also wore a loose white shirt and black denim jeans.

Art took the opportunity to transfer the knife to his left hand and hold out his right.

"Art Dunham," he said.

After a moment's startled hesitation, the turbaned man took the offered hand and replied, "Mehmet Karagöz."

"Pleased to meet you," Art said.

"Thank you; it is an honor," Karagöz answered, dropping Art's hand. "May I?" He gestured at the knife.

"Of course."

Karagöz took the dagger and studied it carefully.

"It is not mine," he said at last, handing it back, "but it is assuredly a fascinating item."

More of the Bringers had arrived—though as always, Art hadn't seen them enter. He began to wonder about some secret entrance somewhere; had they cut a new door in the wall or something?

Wherever they had come from, they were interested in the knife, and he found himself passing it around, like a kid at show-and-tell.

At least this got him introduced to the remaining members of the group; the obese Oriental was Wang Yuan, the aging black woman was Tituba Smith, and the herculean black man was Mr. Rabbitt—no first name was given, and Art found himself without the nerve to ask.

None of them recognized the dagger, leaving him as baffled as ever about its origins.

While Granny Yeager and Dr. Torralva were studying it, Art took the opportunity to remark to Innisfree, "I tried to look up Merton Ambrose at the library, and couldn't find a thing."

Innisfree's mouth quirked. "I am not surprised," he said, his accent definitely Scottish for the moment.

"No?"

Innisfree looked sideways at Art for a moment, studying him. "I suppose I should explain, Arthur."

Art did not reply, but simply looked at Innisfree, his eyebrows raised expectantly.

Innisfree sighed.

"The Bringers of Wonder," he said, "are perhaps more nearly a philosophical society than a thespian troupe—or at least, they once were. And Merton Ambrose held the post I now hold. *The Return of Magic* was his masterwork, but it was only printed privately, not published to the general public. Among us, it's recognized as a classic, I would say, but virtually no one else has ever heard of it, and it can't be found in any ordinary town library."

"Oh," Art said. "Um. Then do you expect much of a crowd for your performance?"

Innisfree seemed surprised by the question; he eyed Art carefully before answering, "I believe those we wish to see it will come to see it, and that will be enough."

"Boy!" Ms. Yeager shouted before Art could think of another question. "Come take your damned gewgaw and get out of our way, we have work to do!"

"Yes, ma'am," he said. He collected the dagger and a few apologetic glances from the others, and headed for the stairs.

Chapter Ten

THAT SESSION was relatively short; Art was called upstairs at seven, and went home for a late dinner. Call for the following day was for six—Art had noticed the trend toward a later and later start, and he entirely approved. Six o'clock meant he ate dinner first, a little early, and arrived at the theater about a quarter to.

The day had not been one of the best he ever had; he had been thinking about driving into Boston, to see if the Boston Public Library had anything about Merton Ambrose, but he had wanted to take Marilyn along for company, and he couldn't find her anywhere.

By the time someone finally told him that she'd gone swimming with Anne and Susan, it was too late to make the trip to Boston by himself. Instead, he had spent the afternoon wandering around town, looking at the shops and watching the tourists and sweating in the heat.

At a quarter to six it was still hot outside, and the inside of the theater was sweltering, but the sky had clouded over and he heard thunder rumbling in the distance as he let himself in. No one was in sight anywhere near the theater, inside or out.

He walked up to the box office and turned on the air conditioning; by the time he had crossed the lobby and reentered the house, the Bringers were all waiting silently for him onstage.

He had actually been expecting that. He accepted without question the mystery of how they all appeared so suddenly and quietly; it had become familiar and contemptible. He waved brusquely to the group as he passed and headed wordlessly for the basement.

There was no point in trying to learn anything about what they were really up to. They weren't going to tell him, and he had other things to do than argue with them. He was in no mood to listen to old Ms. Yeager bitching at him.

He had completed his work on one wall of the prop room the day before; anything that had rotted, rusted, or torn he had pulled out and thrown in the trashcan, and the rest he had sorted out and put away again, using a fat felt-tip marker to label the boxes as clearly as he could.

All the prop guns were in one box, prop swords in another, prop knives in a third—except that that one particular wooden one with the peeling paint had never turned up.

He would have thought that someone had walked off with it, but that would mean that someone else had been down here, and that didn't make sense. No one had been down here while he was here, and the place was locked the rest of the time.

The stupid thing had probably gotten tangled in something and put in the wrong box.

It didn't matter, anyway. He was here because he had to be. It made no difference to him or to anybody else if some moldy old prop was mislaid.

Stepping up onto the steel frame against the stone wall at the outer end of the room, he reached up and pulled an unmarked box off the top shelf.

It was heavier than he expected, and he almost dropped it. Carefully, he held it over his head as he lowered himself to the floor. When he was standing safely on bedrock once again, he lowered the box and opened the flaps.

Junk. Old toys, mostly. He wondered what play they were from.

He reached in and pulled an item out at random, and found himself holding an old *Star Wars* action figure, a worn and battered storm trooper.

He smiled. He'd gotten one of these when he was a kid, when he was five or six years old and they'd just come out. He'd named it Charlie, Charlie the Stormtrooper, and he and Charlie had fought long wars against invisible Nazis on the floor of his bedroom.

He'd lost Charlie years ago, of course.

This one looked just like Charlie. Of course, all these mass-produced figures looked alike, but this one even seemed to be worn in the same places, had the same crooked angle to its head from getting bashed against the headboard of his bed during a brief period of Nazi success.

A coincidence.

He put the storm trooper aside and reached into the box.

A seashell, a shell the size of his fist—just like one he'd picked up on Cape Cod one summer. His father had told him what kind it was, but he didn't remember; a whelk, maybe? Whatever it was, it was about the most intact shell he'd ever found anywhere on the New England coast.

This one looked just like it.

He held it to his ear and listened in wonder to the roar of the sea—though he knew it was really the echo of his own bloodstream pumping.

He lowered it again and stared at it.

What had happened to that old shell of his, anyway? It had disappeared once when he cleaned his room, and never turned up again.

Strange coincidence, the shell and the storm trooper both looking so familiar. He reached into the box again.

When his hand came back out, it slowed, and then stopped, his third discovery dangling before him.

It was Bear.

There was absolutely no possibility of a coincidence or a mistake; this was Bear, the ratty, mildewed teddy bear he had adored as a child, and then relinquished in an impromptu ceremony when he started first grade. The left hind foot was torn, and the pink patch his mother had sewn on had never quite covered the tear; the button eyes didn't match exactly because one was a replacement; a narrow wedge of the dark brown plush was pale gray where bleach had been spilled on it once in the laundry room.

It was, beyond any question, his very own Bear.

What the hell was it doing *here*?

Was this really Charlie, then? And his own lost seashell? He dumped the box out on the floor and began pawing through its contents.

Several minutes later he sat back, confused and furious.

Everything in the box was something he had lost, something that had once been beloved and magical. And practically everything he had ever loved and had lost was in there. There were a few items he didn't really recognize on a conscious level, but they were old, heavily used baby things, and there could be little doubt that they, too, had once been his. A pacifier still had part of his name on it.

What the hell was all this stuff doing here? Who had put it here? Who had collected it all? *How* had they collected it all?

It couldn't have anything to do with the Bringers of Wonder; they wouldn't have known about any of this stuff, or been able to find it.

Had one of his parents found and saved all these old things without telling him? Had his father put the box down here for safekeeping, with the idea of hauling it out someday for the sake of nostalgia?

That didn't sound like his dad at all. He was nostalgic enough, maybe, but he'd have kept everything in the house, and he'd have told Art, he wouldn't have kept it a secret.

And whoever it was—what *right* did they have to muck around with Art's private past?

There were things here he'd have sworn were secret, that no one ever knew he even had—the ragged copy of *Bizarre Sex #9* he'd kept hidden behind his bureau when he was ten, the foil-wrapped condom he'd picked up in the parking area on Hilltop Drive when he was thirteen. How had anyone found those?

And why would anyone collect all this stuff so indiscriminately?

It was crazy. It made him nervous.

He dumped everything back in the box, closed the flaps, and started to carry it back to the high shelf—then stopped.

Why should he put it back up there? After all, this was all *his* stuff. It didn't belong in the theater at all!

He took the box over to the door and set it down. All those lost treasures were going home with him.

And so was one other item, he decided. He got the bone-handled knife from the shelf where he'd left it and put it on top of the box.

That settled, he pulled out the next box, a big one.

For a moment, he hesitated before opening it. What if this box held something else weird and mysterious? What if it held more lost things—someone else's, perhaps? Or an entire set of strange cutlery? Or something even more out of place?

Well, what if it did? It wasn't going to jump out and bite him.

He lifted the flaps and found a stack of cardboard imitations of Roman shields, a remnant of a production of *Julius Caesar* some ten years back. Those went over near the swords, of course.

He found no other oddities that evening.

It was about eleven when Maggie called him. She was waiting at the top of the stairs when he came trudging up, the box of lost treasures under his arm.

"What's that?" she asked.

"Oh, found some things I'd lost," he replied.

She blinked at him, then smiled broadly.

"Already?" she said.

He stared at her, puzzled and angry, as he mounted the last few steps.

"What do you mean, 'already'?" he demanded. "What do *you* know about it? Did you have anything to do with this?"

"No, no," she said, "I didn't mean anything."

"Then why'd you say it?"

"Just . . . I don't know. It popped out. I didn't mean anything." She turned away, toward the stage door.

He glared at her back. So the Bringers were involved after all—but how *could* they be?

"I've been meaning to ask," Art said, trying to hide

his anger, "where are you folks all staying, while you're in town? You don't all live around here, do you?"

"Live around here?" Startled, she turned to look at him. "You mean us?"

"Sure, you know, in Concord or Bedford or wherever—I'm pretty sure none of you are from Bampton, are you?"

"Oh, no, none of us are local." She managed an uneasy little laugh. "We came in from . . . well, from all over."

"That's what I thought," Art said with a nod. "So where are you staying?"

Maggie waved a hand vaguely. "Oh, different places," she said. "I'm rooming with some distant relatives, third cousins or so."

"Oh. Anyone I might know?"

"I don't think so."

"In Bampton?" he persisted.

She hesitated. "I'm not sure," she said.

That was ridiculous, of course; how could she not know what town they lived in? He glowered at her.

As he glowered, he was trying to figure out just how the Bringers could have known about all those lost things. It seemed clear that they must have local people working with them—but who? And why?

The whole thing was just crazy.

"I need to go shut off the air conditioning," he said, putting down the box.

"I'll see you tomorrow, then," Maggie said, smiling. "At seven, this time."

"But tomorrow's Saturday, you can have all day . . ." he began. Then he stopped. "Oh," he said, "do you mean seven in the morning?"

"No, no—seven P.M. In the evening. Even if it is Saturday." She opened the stage door and blew him a kiss, and then she was gone.

Chapter Eleven

THE BOSTON Public Library wasn't any more help than the Bampton library, as far as Merton Ambrose and *The Return of Magic* were concerned, and his car overheated on the drive back. By the time he got home and rushed through a quick meal of leftover chicken it was five past seven.

He wasn't sure whether he expected to find the Bringers of Wonder waiting for him in the parking lot or not; it might be more in character for them to appear mysteriously once he was inside.

In the event, he found Maggie sitting alone on the porch, elbows on her knees, watching the sun set over Old Man Christie's fields. Christie's aging white gelding, Spanner, was in the nearest field, watching her in that vaguely puzzled way horses have. White birds were circling over her head; as Art approached they swooped away and seemed to vanish, like soap bubbles popping, in the shadows of the theater's eaves.

"Hi," he called. "Sorry I'm late."

She turned and smiled. "Hi, Art," she said.

"Where are the others?"

"Oh, they saw you weren't here and went down the street to get a soda or something."

He looked up at the sidewalk, but didn't see any sign of anyone else. "I guess they aren't in any hurry," he said.

"I guess not," Maggie agreed. "After all, everything's been going so well . . ."

"Has it?" Art asked, startled.

"Well, yes," Maggie replied, equally startled by his reaction.

"But it's been almost a week, and you haven't built any of the sets, or hung any lights. Do you have costumes designed, or anything?"

71

"Well, no . . ."

"Then what's going well?"

Maggie hesitated before replying. "The performance," she said at last, "the preparations. I mean, I guess we haven't done much on the . . . the technical side, but we've got the scripts all set, and I think everyone knows his part, just about."

"Really?" He glanced up at the red-painted clapboards behind them. "I hadn't heard anyone rehearsing."

"Have you been listening?"

"Um . . ." Art realized that for the past few days he had been far too busy in the prop room to pay any attention to noises overhead. For that matter, while one could hear what was happening onstage from the big room, from the prop room events upstairs were pretty inaudible.

"I guess not," he admitted.

For a moment they stood silently on the little porch; then Maggie suggested, "Let's go on inside; they'll all be along in a minute, and if I'm not here waiting they'll know to come on in."

"Right." Art fished the key ring from his pocket and unlocked the stage door.

Inside, with the work lights on, he could see that a second, larger white chalk circle had been added to the design on the stage, completely surrounding what had been there before.

"What's that?" he asked.

"What? Oh, that," Maggie said. "That's just so we all know where to stand. See, over there, that red squiggle? That's my place. At the beginning, I mean, when the curtain goes up."

"Blocking marks," Art said.

"I guess," Maggie agreed.

"Sort of funny ones," Art remarked. "Fancier than usual."

Maggie just shrugged.

Blocking marks, learning the script—that sounded normal enough. Maybe the group was legitimate after all, and just had some peculiar approaches to their business. Art looked over at the lighting equipment shelves, in the stage-left wings. "Still haven't done any lighting work," he remarked.

"No," Maggie agreed. "I think we're still working on the staging. I mean, don't we need to know what's going to be where before we light it?"

"Yeah," Art admitted, "you do. But you haven't started building the set, either—are you going to *have* a set?"

"The show doesn't call for much of one," Maggie explained. "It's mostly supposed to take place in a single room, on a single night."

"Still seems like you'd want to get that done and out of the way," Art muttered.

Maggie shrugged again.

"What about costumes?" Art asked. "Did you people bring those with you?"

"Some of us," Maggie admitted. "I haven't got mine yet, though."

Art nodded.

Maggie was being relatively informative tonight, he thought, and in fact, everything was looking somehow far more normal than it had all week. Blocking marks, learning lines, going out for a drink before getting started, that was all the sort of thing he expected. He found himself feeling generous.

"If you like," he said, "you can come down and look through the costumes downstairs, see if you find something you like. What sort of part is it?"

Maggie smiled wryly. "Oh, I play a witch," she said. "Of course."

Art smiled back. "I'd have expected old Ms. Yeager to play that part."

"She's the *old* witch, silly," Maggie said, grinning. She poked him in the shoulder. "I'm the *young* witch."

"Oh."

For a moment, the two of them stood there on the stage, looking at one another; Art glanced around at the door, wondering when the others would arrive.

"There are costumes downstairs?" Maggie asked, breaking the silence.

"Sure," Art said. "Wanna see?"

"Lead the way."

Art did just that.

The first costume room was on the north side of the central passageway, next to the stairway and across from the prop room; the ancient paneled door was painted green, with a cardboard sign held on by thumbtacks, ink that had once been black but was now faded to pale gray on a card that had once been white but was now brown and speckled.

WARDROBE, it said.

This wasn't the only room that held costumes, but the others were considered dead storage; all the good stuff was supposed to be in this one. After some experimentation, Art found the appropriate key; he opened the door and groped for the light switch.

Maggie pushed the door wide as the light came on, and stared in.

A lone bare bulb cast yellow light on a long, narrow room; to either side a steel pipe extended from end to end at about eye level, with dozens, perhaps hundreds of costumes and empty hangers hooked over it. Both pipes sagged in the center from the weight of the clothing. Above each pipe ran a single long shelf, stacked with hats and hatboxes. The room's far wall was rough stone painted white; centered in the stone was a small black door, of normal width but only about five feet high.

Maggie stepped in and ran her eye down the row of costumes on the left, then turned and looked over the row on the right. There were gowns and robes galore, and several bodysuits of plush or velour for use in simulating animals. There were cheap imitations of tuxedoes, cut correctly but made of thin cotton; opera capes, togas, doublets, and various period garments. Velvets, silks, sequins, and gold braid abounded.

"I don't see anything really witchy," Maggie said. "What's through there?" She pointed at the black door.

Art followed the pointing finger and stared, baffled.

He had seen the door when they entered, of course, and surely he had seen it before, whenever he came into the wardrobe room, but somehow he didn't remember it.

Where *could* it go? That was an outside wall; anything beyond it would be under the parking lot.

"I don't know," he admitted.

"Really?" Maggie turned to stare at him.

Art shrugged. "Really," he said.

Maggie marched down the length of the room, grabbed the knob, and tried to turn it.

"Locked," she said.

Art was curious now. How had he missed ever noticing that door, in all the years he had hung out in the theater?

"Hang on a minute," he said. "I've got all the keys here; let's see if one of them will open it." He marched up beside her and began trying keys.

None of them fit.

He went through the entire ring twice without finding a single one that would fit in the keyhole. Finally, disgusted, he flung the entire ring against the wall. It struck with a jangle, and fell to the floor; he glowered at it.

"Well, it's not important," Maggie told him.

"Yes, it is," he protested. "I'm supposed to know what's going on around here, and I don't. I don't remember any door in here, and I'm supposed to have a key for every door and I don't have a key for this one, and there are things in the prop room that shouldn't be here—just what the hell is going on here, anyway?"

"I don't . . . I don't know," she said, taken aback.

"And then there's you people," he shouted, turning all his accumulated anger and frustration on her. "You appear out of nowhere, come and go mysteriously, like a bunch of spies or something, you're putting on a play nobody ever heard of that you haven't started advertising with just three weeks to go, you've got no sets, no lights, you're a dozen of the most strangely assorted people I've ever seen, you won't say where you're staying, you won't let anyone watch you do anything—just what the hell is the big mystery, anyway, lady?''

Maggie blinked back tears.

"I can't tell you," she whispered.

"Why *not*?" he demanded.

"I can't tell you that, either."

"Oh, hell." He scooped up the key ring. "Look, you people just have fun tonight, okay? I'm going to leave you all to your own devices. You can find your own witch costume. I'm going out for a walk, and if you finish up before I get back, use the phone by the lightboard to call my house, and either I'll be there or someone will take a message." He turned, and stamped away, down the passage and up the stairs.

The Bringers of Wonder were on the stage, standing in a ring around the chalk circles, arguing about something. He paid no attention as he stamped out, slamming the door behind him.

Outside, the sun was down, and the sky was the deepening liquid blue of summer twilight. Three white birds, startled by the slam of the door, fluttered out from under the eaves and soared away on the evening breeze.

He stared after them. Where had *they* come from? He had never noticed any birds nesting there, and certainly not any like those. They weren't seagulls or pigeons—they were smaller than gulls, more graceful than pigeons; he couldn't place them.

His anger dissipating, he marched down the steps to the asphalt.

To the west the last glow of sunset gleamed above the treetops on Christie's little farm—if you could really call it a farm. Two acres of pasture, chicken coops, and vegetable gardens, inhabited by an old man, two horses, and a dozen hens—not much of a farm, but the closest thing left in Bampton. Spanner was still out in the field, quietly cropping grass in the gathering gloom; his companion, little Sparkle, was nowhere to be seen.

To the north was a row of quiet little houses, his family's own among them; to the south was the center of town, where the tourists passed through and sometimes stopped on their way to more interesting places, and where the locals did their shopping when it wasn't worth a trip to the Burlington Mall.

It was a quiet, pleasant place, Bampton was; Art was used to that, and he liked it that way. If he wanted excitement or confusion, he could go into Boston or Cambridge.

What were these people doing, these Bringers of Wonder, bringing their mysteries here?

He looked east, out toward Thoreau Street, along the side of the theater. Black asphalt shingles along the roof, red-painted eaves, red-painted clapboards, down to the whitewashed stone of the foundation—where could that door go? It would have to come out under the parking lot, but there *wasn't* anything under the parking lot.

It didn't make any sense.

Maybe it didn't go anywhere; maybe it was a fake, a practical joke. Or maybe it opened into a tiny little clothespress, inside the stone foundation wall.

He couldn't figure it out, and after a moment he stopped trying and just started walking.

Chapter Twelve

"DAD?"

Art's father looked up from his magazine. "Hi, Art," he said. "They quit early tonight?"

"No."

The elder Dunham glanced at his watch. "It's only eight-thirty," he said. "Seems early to me."

"They didn't quit yet. I walked out. I'll go back to lock up later, I guess."

His father put down the magazine and sighed. "What's the problem? They doing something illegal, or dangerous, or something?"

"No, it's nothing like that," Art said. "Just a . . . a personality conflict, I guess. I felt like . . . well, there have been some weird things happening, and I need to think, so I took a walk."

Paul Dunham looked at his son silently for a moment. "Okay," he said at last, "but I hope this isn't going to be a regular thing; I want you in there, keeping an eye on the place."

"I don't do all that much of that anyway, Dad; I spend half my time in the basement while they're doing mysterious secret stuff."

Dunham frowned.

"Anyway," Art said, "there was something I wanted to ask you about."

"What?"

"That door in the wardrobe room, the room next to the stairs, the black door in the outside wall—none of the keys you gave me will open it."

Art's father frowned again, this time more puzzled than annoyed. "What door?" he asked.

"In the basement, in the first storeroom on the left, with all the old costumes on hangers."

Dunham thought for a second, then said, "I don't know what door you're talking about. There should be keys for all the doors on that ring."

"Well, I couldn't find a key to fit that one."

Dunham sat for a moment longer, staring at Art, then asked, "What do you want me to do about it? I don't know what door you're talking about, or why you want it open at all."

Art explained, "Maggie Gowdie—she's one of Innisfree's people—anyway, Maggie and I were downstairs looking to see if we had a costume that would fit—she plays a witch—and she asked if there were more costumes on the other side of this black door, and I don't remember ever even seeing the door there before. I tried to open it, tried every key on the ring, and none of them fit.''

"There isn't any door there," Dunham said.

"That's what *I* thought, but we saw it."

His father stared at him for another moment, then stood. "Come on," he said, "show me."

They could hear the Bringers' voices even before they reached the porch steps, but could not make out words; father and son looked questioningly at each other. Normally, one could not hear much through the theater walls.

Art shrugged and opened the stage door, and they heard Kier Kaye shouting, "... *isn't working*, Merle!"

Several other voices chimed in, as Innisfree tried to reply and Art stepped in. He glanced back at his father, who waved him on without saying anything.

They crossed the stage-right wings to the basement door as the Bringers continued to argue among themselves, but then, as Art grasped the knob, the argument suddenly ended. In the abrupt silence the click of the latch was clearly audible.

Startled, the Dunhams turned to face the Bringers, and the Bringers turned to see the Dunhams.

A rain of pink and red flower petals was settling softly and noiselessly to the stage, and to the hems of dresses and the laces of shoes and the seams of pants; Art did not see where they had come from.

Maggie was not dressed as a witch, nor was anybody else in a recognizable costume, though Granny Yeager still wore her kerchief and Karagöz his turban.

" 'Scuse us," Art said. "Small problem in the basement."

The Bringers stared at him, and then at each other, as Art led his father down the basement stairs. By the time they reached the landing the Dunhams could hear voices behind them, speaking again but no longer shouting.

In the wardrobe room, the instant Art flipped the light switch Paul Dunham stopped dead in his tracks and stared.

"Son of a bitch," he said.

Art didn't say anything; he waited.

"Now, how the hell did I ever miss noticing that?" the elder Dunham asked himself aloud. "Art, I swear I never saw a door there before, but there it is."

"I had the same reaction," Art said.

"None of the keys will open it?"

"Nope."

For a moment longer, Art's father stared at the black door. Then he asked, "Where does it *go*?"

"I was hoping you could tell me," Art said.

Dunham shook his head. "Art," he said, "it's a complete mystery. I mean, it's obviously always been there, but I swear I never saw any door there before this minute. Son of a bitch. Must've been something hanging in front of it or something."

"So what do we do about it?" Art asked. "Do we hire a locksmith?"

"Yeah," Dunham said, "I guess we do. It's not an emergency—they charge extra for weekends—but Monday morning, first thing."

Art nodded.

"Arnie Wechsler's good," Dunham said. "That's who I've always used in the business. You want to call him, or should I?"

"I'll call, I guess," Art said.

"Good." Still staring at the mysterious door, Dunham began backing out of the room. "Guess I'll leave it up to you, then, and get on home."

"Okay." Art decided against accompanying his father; after all, he still had to lock up after the Bringers left. And he wanted to talk to them, anyway—or at least to Maggie.

Maybe he could do that immediately; the Bringers hadn't

80

looked as if they were doing anything terribly secret. "I'll walk you upstairs," he said.

Together, the two ascended the steps.

Innisfree was waiting for them at the top. Behind him, onstage, the other eleven Bringers stood watching.

"Mr. Dunham," Innisfree said, spreading his hands. "An unexpected pleasure to see you here, a real delight!" His accent was almost Cockney this time.

"Mr. Innisfree," Dunham said. "I was, ah, just checking on something downstairs."

Innisfree smiled. "And is all in order and as it should be?"

"I'm not sure," Dunham admitted, "but it isn't anything to worry about."

"Well, that's good, that's *fine*, then."

Dunham stared at the smiling magician. "Was there something you wanted?" he asked.

"Well," Innisfree said apologetically, "I'm afraid it's your son I need to speak to."

Dunham glanced quickly at Art, who shrugged ever so slightly.

"I'll get on home, then," Dunham said. "Call if you need me."

"Okay, Dad."

Dunham waved to the others as he walked across to the stage door. He hesitated, looking back at his son and the tall foreigner. Innisfree smiled, and Art waved good-bye.

Then Dunham was gone, out into the warm summer night, and Art turned to face Innisfree.

"Is there a problem?" He wondered whether Maggie had said anything about his storming out.

"You might say so, yes," Innisfree said; he was eyeing Art contemplatively, as if trying to determine not the best way to say what he had to say, but rather, how much to tell.

"I've been staying out of your way," Art said.

"Indeed you have, lad, and therein lies the problem."

Art blinked.

"It seems we misjudged our capacities, and we do, indeed, need your help," Innisfree said. He paused, and quickly amended that. "Or at least, we might."

"Um . . . just what did you have in mind?"

"Oh, we merely ask that you not leave the building during our rehearsals. Working in the cellars is fine; we can find you there easily enough. When you took your walk tonight, though—well, it was worrisome."

"Worrisome?" Art looked around, puzzled. The other Bringers were still just standing there, watching the conversation—didn't they have anything better to do?

Perhaps they didn't. "Was there something you needed help with?"

"Oh, we managed, we managed," Innisfree said hastily. "We just wanted to ask you not to leave the building during our rehearsals."

Art stared at the tall man, trying to figure this out.

The Bringers of Wonder had, right from the first, made it absolutely clear that they didn't want any outsiders around, and that outsiders included Art. Now they said they needed him to be in the building.

Anywhere in the building?

And they weren't asking him to help with anything. They just wanted him in the theater.

Did that make any sense at all?

No.

This might finally be a chance to find out just what the heck was going on, though.

Or maybe not; maybe it was just as they said.

"I don't understand," he said. "Do you want me to help out or not? Because if you don't, what difference does it make where I am?"

"Well, we want you close by, just in case," Innisfree said with a smile.

"So how about if I get some fresh air in the parking lot?"

The smile vanished.

"We'd prefer it if you stayed inside the building."

"Well, but I don't feel like going back downstairs—it's sort of musty down there, and my allergies are acting up." This was a lie; Art had no allergies.

Innisfree glanced over his shoulder at the others.

"I could sit and watch," Art suggested.

When Innisfree didn't answer immediately, he added, "And once I've seen the play, I could help with lighting it—I notice you haven't started rigging lights yet."

Innisfree sighed.

"We're not ready for that yet," he said. "Perhaps, if not the basement, there's something to be done out in the lobby?"

Art considered.

"All right," he said, "I can find something, I'm sure."

Innisfree smiled again. "Fine! That's fine, then! Thank you, Arthur, my lad!"

"No problem." He closed the basement door, checked the lock, and made his way slowly up the center aisle.

He could feel a dozen pairs of eyes watching him.

He wondered whether Innisfree knew what he was doing. Did these people not want someone watching just because it would make them nervous, or was there something they really didn't want him to see?

If the latter, they'd just blown it, because in the little corridor behind the box office was a peephole with a clear view of the stage. It was there so that ushers could let latecomers in without interrupting anything important, so that actors making entrances from the rear would know when to appear—it was a normal and obvious feature of the theater. Ordinarily, he would never have used it to spy on the Bringers, if they had simply told him they didn't want anyone watching, but all this nonsense about not leaving the building, and sending him out to the lobby . . .

Well, if they didn't have the sense to realize he might be able to watch from there, it wasn't *his* fault.

He smiled to himself, and almost skipped the last few steps.

He was finally going to see them rehearse *The Return of Magic*.

Chapter Thirteen

IT WAS odd to see the stage lit only by the work lights from here—usually, he would only use the peephole much further along, after the lights were up. Everything was dim and bare.

"Places, everyone!" Innisfree called. Voices did not carry very well through the peephole, but Art could hear that clearly enough.

Except for Innisfree himself, the Bringers dispersed, to the wings and far upstage—Art wondered whether there would be sets of some kind hiding the three who now stood along the back of the theater, right against the plank wall.

Innisfree stood center stage, facing away from his audience—the audience he presumably didn't know was there. Art shifted his feet slightly; he expected to be watching for some time yet, and he didn't want to get stiff.

The tall man on the stage raised his hands and spoke a word, a word Art had never heard before and could not begin to spell; abruptly, Innisfree's white shirt and light gray slacks vanished, replaced by a floor-length white robe.

Art blinked.

That was a very good stunt; he had no idea where the robe had been hidden, or how Innisfree had gotten it on so quickly without a single snag or jerk.

Then Innisfree began chanting. This time the words weren't *quite* as strange, but they still weren't English; Art thought the language might be Latin.

Other voices joined his, and four of the Bringers stepped forward—Faye Morgan and Al Tanner to stage left, Wang Yuan and Kier Kaye to stage right. They moved inward in slow steps, stopping at the inner circle, forming a ring around Innisfree.

They were wearing robes, gold and red and green and blue. Each of them was holding something. Morgan raised what she held, and Art saw that it was a sword—and at least from where he stood, it didn't look like a prop. It seemed to catch the light amazingly well.

She waved it slightly, and the tip of the sword drew a flaming red line in the air, a line that hung there, burning. She twisted it back on itself and formed it into a symbol, something resembling an infinity sign, but not exactly that, something a little more complex.

Art blinked, and took a moment to rub his eyes.

How did she *do* that?

Wang held up a bone, and etched a symbol in the air; this one blazed white.

Kaye used a gnarled black staff, and her sign glowed green.

Tanner's shape, drawn with something that Art couldn't make out, something that glittered like glass, burned gold.

The lights dimmed.

Art started; how did they do *that*? None of the work lights were on dimmers! The backstage lights never had been, and he'd patched the onstage work lights back out onto the regular toggle switch so they'd be handier for the Bringers.

Were they running some kind of heavy equipment that was draining current? Maybe they'd blown a fuse before, maybe that was the emergency they'd wanted him for.

The other seven Bringers stepped forward now, forming an outer circle; they were still in their street clothes, and they didn't join in the chanting. Some held things, some did not. Maggie stumbled over something, and Art thought he could hear Yeager's penetrating voice muttering.

The lights returned to normal, and the four symbols in the air vanished in wisps of smoke. Innisfree, still standing at center stage with his arms spread, called out, "Behold, our arts are mighty!"

"Nay, Lord," replied Morgan, "they fade, they die!"

"See, Master," Tanner said, "where once we brought forth dragons!"

A pigeon appeared in the air before him, flapping wildly. Art was mildly impressed; he couldn't imagine where the bird had come from. It wasn't anywhere near so fine a trick as the writing-in-air stuff, though.

"See, Magister," Kaye announced, "where once we devastated kingdoms!" A flash of fire sprang from her fingers and vanished in the air.

Art had seen Tanner do that, or something very similar, once before. Maybe Tanner and Kaye had switched roles?

"Sire," Wang said, "our powers dim!"

"That's more like it," Yeager said—not in a theatrical proclamation like the others, but just speaking normally. Her harsh voice cut through the mysticism and shattered the illusion the play had created; Art shook his head in annoyance at being yanked out of the dream.

Onstage, Innisfree dropped his post and nodded. "It's working again," he said. "We don't need to run through all of it right now."

"You're sure it's that young man who's responsible?" Karagöz asked.

Innisfree shrugged. "What else could it be?"

"But he's not . . ." Maggie began.

"Oh, he's not doing it on *purpose*," Innisfree interrupted.

Art blinked. Not doing *what* on purpose?

This was all very interesting. There apparently really was a play being put on, and he had just watched a scene from it—the opening, perhaps? And they had costumes and props, at least some of them, even if they didn't have lights or sets.

They had special effects, too—amazingly good ones. That writing-in-the-air stuff was really something.

They weren't drug dealers or white slavers or anything else reprehensible, after all; Marilyn's theorizing had been wrong. They were a bunch of magicians putting on a show, just as they'd said all along.

But what was he supposed to be responsible for? Why did they want him in the building, but not watching? What was he doing, not on purpose?

"All right, people," Innisfree said, clapping his hands together in a gesture Art thought every director who had ever lived must have used, back at least as far as Aristophanes. "Let's see what we can do." Innisfree looked around, then pointed at Kaye.

She smiled, and vanished in a flurry of green silken robe. A large black cat appeared in her place.

Innisfree's gaze fell on Wang, who raised a hand. Wang held it over his head for a moment; something seemed to shimmer.

Then he lowered it again and shook his head.

"All right, all right," Innisfree said. "It's still early, still three weeks to go."

Art stared at the cat, which was behaving very calmly for a beast that had presumably just been flung onto an open stage by some hidden device. The animal was sitting there, watching Innisfree and the others; it wasn't even washing itself or curling up, it was just sitting there.

And where had Kaye gone, anyway? He hadn't seen any of the Bringers checking the traps or anything. If she was down in the basement . . .

Something orange and white strolled out onto the stage; at first Art thought it was another cat, but then he got a better look at it.

It was a fox. A red fox.

He stared; how on earth had that got there? He'd never heard of anyone taming or training a *fox*.

The word reminded him of something, and he looked at the Bringers.

Ms. Kaye was still missing, and now so was Ms. Fox.

These people were *good*, he decided. If he didn't know better, he would have sworn that Kier Kaye had actually transformed herself into a black cat, and Ms. Fox into a red fox.

The fox and the cat watched each other, but neither made any hostile move—and that, in itself, was pretty amazing. The fox settled down on its haunches a yard or so from the cat and looked about with interest.

Flowers were raining onto the stage, and Art had been so intent on the animals that he had no idea who was responsible. Pink blossoms were falling and drifting from nowhere.

A sudden wind stirred them up, disrupting the slow, gentle swirls and sending petals and stems skittering across the stage. Even from the far end of the house, on the other side of the little peephole, Art could feel the sudden change in the theater's air; it had turned cold and dry, and the wind was increasing.

Art pulled away. What kind of wind machine could do *that*?

And he hadn't seen any wind machine, anyway. The theater didn't come with one; previous productions had borrowed household fans when they needed wind. He hadn't seen one backstage anywhere.

He felt a chill that wasn't just from the cool breeze now spraying out through the peephole.

People onstage were applauding.

This was crazy.

Art marched to the double doors connecting the lobby to the house and swung them wide.

For an instant, he felt that cold, impossible wind; then it died away, and the warm, dead air of the theater was just as still as ever. A hush fell as everyone onstage turned to look at him.

The fox ran for the wings; the cat watched him with interest, but did not immediately flee.

"Arthur!" Innisfree called. "Was there something you wanted?"

There were flowers and loose petals strewn all over the stage; he had not imagined that. The cat was still there, staring at him; he had not imagined *that*, either.

But what could he say?

Could he say, "I think your magic is too real," or, "You're frightening me," or, "What are you doing?"

"I'm done up here," he said. "Thought I'd check the fuses; it seemed like the lights dimmed a minute ago."

The cat got up and ambled off, stage right.

"Suit yourself," Innisfree said. "Can't say as I noticed anything."

Art strolled down the aisle, hands in his pockets, determinedly casual, as the Bringers stood about, watching him or doing nothing. They looked just as sincerely casual as he did, he realized; all ten of them looked as if they were nervous and trying to hide it.

Eleven of them, that is; Ms. Fox reappeared as he reached the front row. And twelve; when he mounted the stage-right steps, Ms. Kaye emerged from the wings.

He scuffed at the flowers as he crossed the stage; they were real and solid. He glanced around.

The five who had formed the inner circle—Innisfree, Wang, Kaye, Morgan, and Tanner—were still in their robes, but the props had vanished. He could see no sword, no staff, no bone, no bottle.

And there wasn't any wind machine anywhere. He even glanced up at the catwalk, but no, that was empty.

The main fuse box looked just fine, but that was reasonable enough; it was designed for about 15,000 watts of stage lighting, could handle 20,000 in a pinch, and the work lights and a few special effects wouldn't bother it.

Not unless the special effects were drawing a *lot* of current, in which case they'd be a serious fire hazard. Art frowned at the thought, then shook his head.

There weren't any cords or cables; nobody was drawing extra current from this box. The work lights had their own two circuits, each with a thirty-amp screw-in fuse, and those weren't smoked or hot, let alone blown.

If there'd been enough draw to dim the lights the fuses should have at least been warm to the touch, and they weren't.

One of these days, Art thought, he'd have to talk his father into putting in circuit breakers; it was getting hard to find the old-fashioned fuses.

On the other hand, a circuit breaker didn't get warm or smoked, did it? It was either tripped or it wasn't, where fuses could show warning signs.

And he was thinking about this to keep from thinking about anything else. He knew he was doing it. The rest of it was too hard to deal with. Where had the wind come from? The flowers? The fox? Why did they want him in the building?

They weren't drug dealers or white slavers, but they might still be cultists, and right now he wouldn't put it past them to be using *real* magic and wanting him for their ritual sacrifice.

Except there's no such thing as magic, he reminded himself. There couldn't be.

It was just a lot of things adding up, all getting to him at once, that made him even consider the possibility of real magic, he told himself. He knew better than that. If he weren't by himself in the theater, surrounded by weirdos, at night . . .

"Looks okay here," he said.

"Isn't there another fuse box in the cellars?" Maggie asked.

Startled, he turned to look at her, and found all twelve of the Bringers watching him.

"Yeah, there is," he admitted. "I'll go take a look."

They watched him cross the stage, watched him fumble with the keys and get the basement door open; it was with a great rush of relief that he took the first step down, out of their sight.

He emerged into the passage at the bottom and was unable to resist the temptation; he turned right and slid the big door open and turned on the light in the big room under the stage.

Nothing had been disturbed; the traps in the ceiling were all closed, and showed no signs of recent use.

He shrugged and turned around.

The prop room looked just as he had left it.

The wardrobe room was just as he remembered; the black door was still there, still closed and mysterious.

He ambled down the corridor to the end, and turned left, into the narrow passageway where the water meter and the lobby fuse box resided. This space was in deep shadow; the only light came from the ceiling lights in the central passageway, and the last of those was about ten feet back from the corner. Art's own body blocked out much of the light.

He could make out the pull-chain of the passage's own light, though; he reached up and gave it a tug. The bare bulb that hung down to a few inches above his head came on.

On the left was cracking plaster, painted white long ago, now faded to a dull gray; the lath beneath had patterned the gray with darker two-inch stripes.

On the right the wall was rough stone, the last remnants of ancient whitewash still visible in streaks here and there; black pipes emerged from the stone near the ceiling, turned a right angle, and descended the wall to eye level, where they connected to the rusted green metal box of the water meter. Farther in, near the corner, was the black steel of the fuse box, two thick metal-wrapped cables leading out the top and into the ceiling. The ceiling, far above, was bare planking, dark with age; the floor was gray granite.

And the far end of the passageway was another rough stone wall—but in this one was a door. A black six-panel door, full-sized, its ancient finish crazed and pebbled, speckled with the orange of old shellac.

"Oh, my God," Art said, staring.

There had never been a door there before. He *knew* that. There were never any costumes stored here that might have hidden it.

He fished out his key ring, just in case, and stepped forward into the passage. With the ring in his left hand, he reached out with his right and gripped the blackened brass knob.

It turned. The latch clicked, and the door swung open.

And warm sunlight spilled into the corridor around him.

At 10 P.M., in a New England cellar, sunlight lit the passage, colored his sneakers with gold.

He blinked, and stepped through the door.

Chapter Fourteen

MAGGIE SAW the light the moment she stepped into the central corridor.

"Art?" she called, as she made her way step by step down the passage. "Art, are you there?"

She hesitated at the corner, then turned, and found the open door.

And Art.

He was sitting in a meadow, surrounded by golden flowers and dancing butterflies. The sun hung huge and orange in the west; he was facing it, watching it.

Maggie approached cautiously, but he heard her somehow, and looked up, startled. He said something, but she couldn't hear it—which came as no surprise, really. She had never seen such a door before, but she had heard of them and knew something about how they worked. The moment she had seen the meadow she had known what she faced, and that knowledge was itself something of a shock, but once that was past mere details were nothing.

She hesitated again on the threshold, then stepped through.

In an instant, the silence of the theater basement was replaced with the whirring of insects and the singing of the birds that pursued them. A gentle breeze rippled through the grass and flowers.

She turned quickly, and made certain that the door was still there, still open.

It was; its frame was part of a small, colorful little shed built against the side of a steep hill. The shed was enamel and gilt and painted porcelain, but through it she could see the rough stone and plaster of the basement corridor, the fuse box, the water meter, all of it sane and normal.

"Maggie," Art said. "Sit down."

"I don't know if . . ."

"Sit down!" Art bellowed.

Maggie sat down quickly.

For a moment, the two of them sat there in the grass, staring at each other. Art's expression was blank, and Maggie's wary.

Then Art spoke, saying wearily, "Maggie, whoever you are, will you tell me something?"

"What?" she asked.

"What the hell is going on?" He waved an arm at the landscape, taking in the meadow, the sinking sun, the grove of trees nearby, the towers that glittered above the trees in the distance. "What *is* this place?"

Maggie sighed.

"I suppose," she said, "that I'll have to tell you everything."

"Please," Art said.

"I told you I'm a witch . . ." she began.

"No," he corrected her, "you told me that your grandmother had been called a witch."

"All right, you're right, I did," she agreed. "Well, whatever I told you, I *am* a witch. A real one, and the last real Scottish witch in the world."

"Wiccan, you mean? There aren't any in Scotland?"

"No, not Wiccan. They're just pagans. I mean, some of them *think* they're witches, but . . ." Her voice trailed off. She paused, then said, "Let me start over."

"By all means," Art agreed.

"This is magic," she said, waving an arm to take in the entire landscape that surrounded them. "It's *real* magic, the stuff that's in all the old stories."

"It's not a fake, like the holodeck on *Star Trek*?" Art asked. "Or some kind of amusement park, or teleportation, or something?"

"No," Maggie said, "it's magic. This is Faerie."

"I didn't really think it was fake," Art said. "It's too real." He plucked a blade of grass and crumpled it between his fingers.

A thought struck Maggie as she watched, and she asked him, "You haven't eaten anything, have you? Chewed on a bit of grass or anything?"

"No," he said. "It didn't seem like a good idea."

"Good. Don't."

Art nodded. When Maggie didn't immediately continue with her explanation, he asked, "If this is Faerie, where are the fairies, or elves, or whatever it is that lives here?"

"Shh!" Maggie looked around, worried, but spotted nothing nearby save butterflies and flowers. In the shadows of the trees a few fireflies were rising, like sparks from a fire. The birds were settling in for the night. Nothing larger than a meadowlark could be seen moving.

Slightly reassured, she said, "I don't know. I don't *want* to know. I've never been here before, any more than you have; nobody's been able to find a way into Faerie since long before I was born. Nobody knows what's happened in Faerie since . . . well, since about the First World War, I guess. So maybe the locals are hiding, maybe they've forgotten what humans are, or maybe they're just minding their own business. I don't know. I haven't been here, I've just heard about it.''

''So why have you heard about it, and I haven't?'' Art asked, a bit plaintively. ''Why hasn't anyone been here in so long? Why wasn't that door ever there before?''

''Because . . .'' She sighed. ''Because magic is dying. Just like in the play.''

''Why?'' Art asked. ''Because nobody believes in it anymore, like Tinkerbell?''

''No,'' Maggie said, annoyed. ''You've got it backwards, just like people always do. People don't believe in magic anymore because there hardly is any magic to believe in. It's wearing out, getting old and weak. It's been declining for centuries, for millenia, maybe. Whether you believe in it or not doesn't make any difference in whether it works, any more than it matters whether you believe in electricity when you turn on a light—the magic is still there, and still real. But you need to believe in it to *control* it, you need to know which switch to flip. And if you believe in it, it can control *you*, sometimes . . . it's complicated.

''So explain it. I'm listening.''

She glared at him, took a deep breath, and began.

''Magic comes from two things, from people and from places; everybody who knows anything about it knows that there are places of power, that magic works better some places than other, and everybody knows that magic works better for some people than for others, and the more you know about it, the better it works. That's why the old wizards studied it endlessly. And the people grow old and wear out and eventually die—they may stretch their time out with the magic, but they get older and weaker, like anybody else.

''Well, the places get old and die, too. The Valley of the Kings, in Egypt—it's been dead for thousands of years, all that's left is the memories. Mount Fuji's been dead longer than that, no one even remembers why it was holy. Delphi's gone, Angkor Wat is gone, Obersalzburg is gone.

Stonehenge is just stones now, the magic there is an echo of an echo. And . . . well, I won't go through the whole list, but there's only one left, in Sedona, Arizona. All the magic that remains on Earth comes from the American Southwest—and that one's old and weak, too. It'll probably be gone by next year.''

Art started to say something, to ask a question, then thought better of it.

''And the people have been getting scarcer and weaker, too,'' Maggie continued. ''With so few places to draw on, so little strength left, there *can't* be many true magicians, and we can't do as much. And now we're all that's left—just the twelve of us. All the others, the psychics and miracle workers and so-called witches, they're frauds and charlatans. There are just the twelve.''

''The Bringers of Wonder?''

Maggie nodded. ''That's what Myrddin calls us. Twelve of us left, in all the world.''

''Who's Meer-Then?''

''Mr. Innisfree. Myrddin's his real name.''

Art considered that, and accepted it. ''And all the magic you people do is real?'' he asked.

She nodded again.

''So why are you here?'' Art asked. ''I mean, why are you in Bampton?''

''To bring the magic back,'' Maggie said.

Art blinked. ''You can do that?'' he asked.

Maggie hesitated, then answered, ''I don't know.''

Art waited.

''You see, there's this spell,'' she said. ''Or sort of a spell. A ritual, anyway. Someone came up with it long ago—I don't know exactly, some time in the Dark Ages, I guess.''

''What's it supposed to do?''

''What it does—well, it creates a new magical place, a new source of power. Or opens one up, anyway—I mean, it doesn't *create* the magic so much as it finds it and frees it. And there are only certain places that it can possibly work at any given time.''

"Like Bampton?"

She nodded. "Like Bampton. Right now, the block of Thoreau Street from Concord Avenue to Dawes Road, right here in Bampton, Massachusetts, is the only place on Earth with the potential to become a mystical power spot.''

"Seems pretty unlikely. I mean, why here?''

She shrugged. "Who knows? Magic doesn't always have nice, tidy laws and reasons; it isn't science. Right now, it's here. We can tell that—or some of them can, like Myrddin and Dr. Torralva; I can't do it myself, I don't understand the techniques at all.''

Art was going to protest further when a blood-red butterfly landed on his hand, then flew away again. As he watched it go, he decided not to argue. Whatever the reasons, this was happening, wasn't it?

And why *not* Bampton?

"So you people are here to open up this new power source?''

"Like digging a well,'' she agreed. "Or planting a seed.''

"So you'll do your ritual, and then you'll all scatter again, and that'll be it? There will be a little more magic in the world for you witches and wizards, but the rest of us can just go on as usual?''

Maggie hesitated, then said, "The others would probably want me to lie to you and say yes, but I'm not going to.''

"What do you mean?''

"I mean it's not that simple. I don't think you understand the sort of difference we're talking about here. There hasn't been a new well of magic in thousands of years— not since Biblical times.''

"So?''

"So there won't just be a *little* more magic in the world. There will be a *lot*. All the stupid little magical things people do that don't work anymore, the hexes and good-luck charms—they'll work. At least, the ones that are done right. And there will be spontaneous magic, too, things that just *happen*. And wishing hard enough will make things come true, sometimes. Magic will be so easy that anyone will be able to learn it. Love will be magic again— you people all say it is, but it hasn't really been, not for centuries.'' She sighed. ''We don't know what it'll be like; there aren't any reliable records, and while some of us have been around a long time, none of us is *that* old, we don't remember a world where magic was young.''

For a moment the two of them sat silently side by side, as Art considered this.

It sounded terrifying—all that magic would cause chaos, everything would be changed, everything disrupted. Somehow, though, it didn't seem real. After all, *magic*?

Finally he said, ''Sounds dangerous.''

''It probably is,'' Maggie agreed.

''So why are you doing it?''

''Because the alternative is worse, of course. If we *don't* do it, magic is going to die. Forever.''

''But can't you open one of these wells any time you want?''

She shook her head. ''No, of course not,'' she said. ''It takes magic to make it work, to plant the seed. When Sedona goes—that's it. That's all, for all of time; no more magic, ever. And the old ones, Baba and Myrddin and . . . well, really, everybody but me, magic is all that's keeping them alive. When the magic goes, they'll die, too.''

Art blinked. ''They will?''

She nodded, not looking at him.

''Why'd they leave it until the last minute, then? Why didn't they start a new one a long time ago? If it's been thousands of years . . .''

''Well,'' Maggie said, ''there's a trick to it.''

''What kind of a trick?''

''The spell we're using, the play—it needs to include *all* of the surviving magicians in the world. If any magician, anywhere in the world, doesn't take part, it will fail—not just big-shot wizards, if there's *anyone* else, anywhere, using magic, then it won't work. And there's always been a holdout, some kind of a problem—some hedge witch or tribal shaman somewhere who wouldn't go along, or someone who couldn't come to the right place. That was the big problem, for about the last thousand years—Myrddin was imprisoned in a cave in England. It was just recently that the spell holding him got weak enough, and the rest of us got organized enough, that we could get him out.''

The idea of Innisfree being some ancient wizard who had spent centuries in a cave struck Art as patently ridiculous, and he snickered.

"Really!" Maggie insisted.

"He got that tan sitting in a British cave?"

"No, he got that tan in North Africa," Maggie said. "First thing he did when he got out was go get warm and dry. Wouldn't you? And that's why he picked that name, Innisfree—he's free again. That's why he's so cheerful about everything, and nervous at the same time—he's glad to be out, but he doesn't really understand how the world works anymore.''

"He hides it well."

"It's all bluster."

Art still doubted the whole thing, but every time he looked at the world around him, at the black door in the hillside, the wildflowers all around, the huge sun settling on the horizon when he had already seen the sun set once that day, he had to believe that something utterly incredible was happening, and Maggie's explanation seemed to make just as much sense as anything else.

Maybe it was real.

And if so, shouldn't he be frightened?

"So let's see if I have this straight," Art said. "Magic is dying out, and there are only twelve real magicians left.''

Maggie nodded.

"And you have a way to bring magic back, big time, but you have to do it before the end of the year, and here in Bampton."

"Before the winter solstice, to be exact," Maggie agreed.

"And you found this theater sitting in exactly the right place, so Innisfree rented it, and you're planning to stage your big ritual on the thirtieth, and for now you're all practicing up for it. And you didn't want any outsiders around because you didn't want them interfering."

"Right."

Art nodded. "So if magic is so weak, what are we doing sitting in this field? Where'd that door come from?"

"Well, magic isn't always linear," Maggie explained. "It can spill back and forth through time. And it's already started here, because we're planning the ritual. Also, I think it started on Lammas Night, when you people put on that play, with the fairies in it—that play, on that night, in that place, it probably started loosening things up a little. And all those things in the cellars, charged with imagination and excitement and youthful fervor—the theater's a natural storehouse for magic. Not to mention that it used to be a church. I'll bet I've seen more real magic in the week we've been here than I'd seen in the last ten years."

Art mulled that over, then asked, "So if it's spilling back in time, does that mean you're going to perform the ritual, and it's going to succeed, and nothing can stop you?"

"No." Maggie shook her head. "If something stops us, then that magic will all just be a fluke, a passing whim of the universe, a taste of what might have been. If we don't perform our spell when the moon's back in the same phase it was in on Lammas Night, then our chance is gone. And I don't know if we'll have another before the solstice."

"What's Lammas Night?"

"August first. One of the four nights of power every year. Candlemas, Beltane, Lammas, and Halloween."

"But if I leave you people alone, you'll work your spell, and magic will return?"

Maggie hesitated, then said, "No."

Startled, Art demanded, "Why *not*?"

"That's why we needed you in the building, Art; that's why we're here, now, I think. You're all tangled up in the magic. Maybe it's just because you were there when we started, or maybe it's something more than that, some connection between you and the mystic-place-to-be, but our spells don't work when you're not here. If you aren't in the building when we perform *The Return of Magic*, it won't work. And it's even worse' than that, now that I've told you all this. It isn't just all the magicians in the world who need to work the spell; it's everyone who knows the spell is being attempted. You asked about magic and belief—belief isn't all that important, but *knowledge* is. You know about it, now, and if you don't participate, if you don't act out your consent, it won't work."

She turned and looked him straight in the eye. "Now that I've told you, Art, it's up to you. If you help us, magic will be loose in the world, new, fresh, powerful magic, magic everywhere, magic dripping from the eaves and shining from the windows of every house in Bampton, blossoming and singing, wild and uncontrolled.

"And if you don't help us, all magic will be gone from the world forever, and eleven of us will die.

"So . . ." She swallowed nervously. "So, will you help?"

Chapter Fifteen

ART STARED at her for a moment, then got to his feet. He brushed off the seat of his pants and looked around.

"What happens to all this, though?" he asked. "Isn't this all magic?"

"Of course it is," Maggie agreed, rising. "And if the ritual fails, it'll be gone forever. I'm not sure if it will all cease to exist, or whether it has an independent reality of its own and will just be closed off from Earth forever, but whichever it is, the effect will be the same—that door there will be gone, it'll just be a stone wall again, with nothing on the other side but dirt and granite."

"You're sure of that?"

She shrugged. "As sure as I can be," she said. " 'The essence of magic is deceit'—that's what Heliophagus of Smyrna said. I think maybe he overstated the case, but it's a tricky business, and we're hardly ever sure of *anything*."

"So you aren't *sure* that Innisfree would die?"

Maggie sighed. "Art," she said, "Myrddin is sixteen hundred years old. It's magic that keeps him young. When the magic's gone, he'll die."

"How? Turn to dust, like in a vampire movie?"

"Maybe." Maggie put a hand on his arm. "We don't know. There's always been magic in the world, ever since history began; how can we know what the world will be like without it?"

He turned to face her, startled. "You mean things could be different? For everybody, not just magicians?"

"Art, I *don't know*."

He looked her in the eye, and noticed that her eyes were deep and green. He pulled away.

"You can cast spells, can't you?"

"Some," she admitted. "More here and now than ever before."

"And you want me to help you with this play of yours?"

She nodded.

"So why don't you just enchant me, and *make* me do what you want?"

Maggie hesitated. "We could," she admitted. "*I* could. But Art, magic isn't like electricity or something, it isn't all the same, regardless of where it came from or how it started. Each of the mystic places in the world has its own flavor—or *had*, anyway—depending on how it was created. And Art, we want this one to be clean and wholesome. We want white magic—and believe me, *you* want it to be white magic, if it happens at all. There's been black magic in the world before, too much of it, too often. It's gone now—the Sedona source is clean, almost pure white—but we know what black magic is, what it's like. We don't want that."

"So what?"

"So if there's dissension, if there's coercion, the Bampton source will be tainted. It can never be better than gray, it might be black."

"And you don't want that?"

"Well, most of us don't." She admitted, "I think a couple might not care."

Art immediately thought of Granny Yeager; he doubted she would hesitate an instant over whether the magic was white or black.

"Besides," Maggie added, "we're not sure it would work. An enchantment isn't *really* consent."

Art nodded.

"Let's go back," Maggie said.

Art nodded again, and together they stepped back through the door into the theater basement.

Art paused, and turned back for a final look. The sun was almost down, the trees black silhouettes before it, the first star just visible in the east.

He closed the ancient door and felt the latch click into

place. He stared at it for a long moment, ran a finger over the rough, crumbling finish.

"Hard to believe this isn't real," he said.

"It's real," Maggie said. "It's magic."

He glanced at her, then back at the door. "It looks so old," he said.

"It probably *is* old," Maggie agreed. "It was probably somewhere else before."

"Is that how it works?"

She spread empty hands. "Who knows?" she replied. "The essence of magic is deceit."

The cellars seemed exceptionally dank and gloomy after the fresh air and vivid sunlight of Faerie, and Art hurried to turn off lights and lock up, so as to get back outside. A hot New England night was scarcely going to be as pleasant as twilight in Faerie, but it would be better than the basement.

Maggie accompanied him silently.

There was no sign of the other Bringers when they finally made their way back upstairs; that was no surprise. Art set out to make sure that the air conditioning was turned off and everything as it should be.

When at last he was satisfied, he found Maggie waiting by the stage door. She looked troubled.

"Will you help us?" she burst out.

He stepped past her without answering and put his hand on the knob, then paused.

"I don't know," he said. "I need to think about it." He turned the knob.

Light spilled in, and he blinked in astonishment.

He swung the door wide and looked out at morning light sparkling on the dew in the fields beyond the parking lot.

"We weren't . . ." he began, but he could not finish the thought.

"You aren't up on your fairy tales, are you?" Maggie asked. "Time in Faerie isn't the same as time on Earth. That's what the stories all say, and I guess they were right."

Art looked at his watch, and found it was blinking "12:00" up at him. He stared at it.

Maggie noticed the gesture. Her mouth twisted wryly. "Digital watches, it would seem, don't work in Faerie," she said. "Nobody knew that before."

Art looked at her. "They didn't have digital watches last time anyone went there, huh?"

Maggie nodded. "I hope we only lost the night, and this is still Sunday morning," she said, looking out toward Thoreau Street.

Art blinked, and stared out at the pale sky.

"It's a good thing you didn't eat anything," Maggie remarked as she started down the porch steps.

"Why?" Art asked.

She glanced up at him. "Don't you know?" she said, startled. "If you eat anything in Faerie, you can't return. The door would have vanished, and you'd have spent the rest of your life there."

"The rest . . ."

"Good night, Art. Call tonight is for seven again—at least, if it's still Sunday."

He stood watching as she stepped gracefully over a broken chunk of rock and vanished around the back corner of the theater.

A car cruised by, and in Old Man Christie's field Spanner whinnied.

Magic, Art thought. Real magic. Witches. Fairies.

Real magic.

Real magic, either about to die forever, or about to be reborn.

He felt a chill of terror at the thought—and a stirring of something else, of excitement, of desire. He quickly suppressed it.

The whole situation was too much to absorb right away, he decided. He would, as he had told Maggie, need time to think about it.

He stared at his watch as he descended the steps and started home.

Chapter Sixteen

HE SLEPT until 4 P.M.

When he finally came downstairs the radio was on, and a newscaster was describing the new comet that was gracing the southern skies, talking about how astronomers were puzzled by the suddenness of its appearance.

"Hi there, sleepyhead!" his father called.

Art waved.

"Those folks keep you up late?" the elder Dunham asked.

Art nodded as he passed through on his way to the kitchen.

"What time did you get in?"

"Seven," Art said, as he got a gallon jug of milk from the refrigerator.

His father made a wordless noise of sympathy.

Art wasn't sure just what meal he was eating, but whatever it was, breakfast or lunch or dinner or just a snack, he decided a microwave pizza would do just fine. He found one in the freezer.

He watched the timer on the microwave oven count down, square blue numbers changing as if by magic.

Microwave ovens were pretty magical, weren't they? Art considered that.

His life was full of miracles, really—everyday, commonplace miracles he accepted without a second thought. Frozen pizza, microwave ovens, digital clocks, he didn't know how any of them worked, they all might as well be magic. Why couldn't he learn to live with a little more, if the Bringers brought their ritual off?

But those things weren't *real* magic.

That fairy meadow was *real* magic.

At least, if all that happened, if he hadn't just dreamed the whole thing. He glanced through the living room door.

The Sunday paper, immediately recognizable by the presence of four-color comics, was strewn about.

"It's Sunday, right?" he called. "I mean, I didn't sleep a whole day or anything?"

"It's Sunday," his father replied.

That was reassuring, it fit with his memories. He hadn't lost whole days in Faerie—and he hadn't dreamt all of Saturday, either.

At least, he didn't think so. If he had dreamt it, wouldn't it still be Saturday now?

But the whole thing was beginning to have the *feel* of a dream; that field, the long, slow sunset, the conversation with Maggie Gowdie, it was all starting to seem unreal, like a story he had once heard, or a daydream.

Was it real?

He slugged down milk, straight from the jug. The microwave beeped, and he found a potholder with which to take out the pizza.

The Return of Magic, they called it, and they meant just that—if it was all true. If Maggie hadn't lied, if the conversation had happened, if the meadow was real, if the door was there, if he hadn't imagined the whole thing.

He tried to straighten his thoughts as he ate, but they wouldn't come straight. He couldn't make himself certain of anything at all about anything that had happened since the end of July. The final performance of *Midsummer Night's Dream*, the cast party, cleaning the theater—that all seemed real enough, there was no reason to doubt it, but then Mr. Innisfree had turned up . . .

A wizard, more than a thousand years old?

A dozen magicians, the last magicians in the world, come to Bampton to put on a play that would cast a spell—there was a pun in that, the cast of the play casting a spell.

"I think I'll go over to the theater," he said, brushing crumbs from his lap.

His father looked up. "Okay," he said. "When's call for tonight?"

"Not until six," Art said, shading the truth, "but I wanted to look at something."

"Suit yourself," his father said, returning to his book.

Art took the keys from the hook and left the house.

The air had a heavy, damp feel to it as he clattered down to the sidewalk; he thought it might rain a little later, though you never knew.

The sky was darkening by the time he opened the stage door; rain was now clearly far more likely than not. He flicked on the light and stepped inside.

The chalk circles, white with red symbols, were on the stage, just as he remembered them; the Bringers of Wonder were real, not just a dream, then.

He found his way down the basement stairs, down the central passage, and around the corner at the end. And there, past the water meter and the secondary fuse box, was the door, black and ancient.

He stood in the passageway for a long moment, just staring at it.

Finally, he stepped forward and took the knob gingerly in his hand. He turned it and pulled, half expecting, half hoping, that it would be locked.

It opened easily and silently, and he found himself looking out at the meadow.

It was night in Faerie; the dim glow of the corridor light spilled past him onto dew-moistened grass. Stars shone above the meadows; he leaned forward for a quick look, then hastily pulled back.

Stars, millions of stars, more stars than he had seen since a childhood vacation in the mountains, the Milky Way a white path across the heavens—but all wrong, all in impossible places, the constellations twisted and distorted.

Slowly, carefully, he closed the black door.

It was real.

But was Maggie's story, her explanation of what was happening, was that all true?

What if the Bringers were all the *black* magicians of the world? What if this was some plot?

What if it wasn't really magic at all, what if they were extraterrestrials, and that door was some sort of teleportation device, and they were going to invade and conquer the world? After all, hadn't someone* said that any sufficiently advanced technology is indistinguishable from magic?

He reached out and ran his fingertips over the door, feeling the crazed and beaded finish. It *felt* like the remains of antique varnish, but maybe it was all really some sort of alien microcircuitry.

But the world beyond wasn't alien—it was a *meadow*, with grass and flowers and insects, with Earth's air and gravity . . .

Well, Earth's gravity, anyway; the air might be a trifle richer, might have a different mix of inert gasses for all he could tell.

But what would alien invaders be doing putting on a play? Why would they conjure up birds and flames and winds and flowers? Why would their portal come out in a meadow, and not a city or staging area?

The alien-invader hypothesis had a certain appeal—Art had never even believed in UFOs or psychic phenomena or any of the New Age stuff, let alone full-blown traditional magic, witches and wizards and spells, so any sort of scientific explanation would be welcome, but still, he couldn't really make himself believe it.

It looked like magic. It felt like magic.

And even if it was really some sort of super-science, he might as well *treat* it as magic.

Slowly, thinking deeply, he turned away from the door and ambled back down the central passageway.

When he reached the prop room he glanced at the door, but didn't open it.

The box of lost things—that was magical, wasn't it? They were all things that had felt magical to him once, all things that had been inexplicably lost, and now magic had brought them back to him.

---

* Arthur C. Clarke: Clarke's Third Law, 1940.

White magic, surely. Even when he had had no idea what was going on, even when he had been furious that someone was playing tricks on him with his own lost treasures, he had felt a reawakening of childlike wonder when he had handled those trinkets, all that outgrown junk.

The bone-handled knife—that must be magic, too. He frowned. A knife didn't seem like a good omen.

He opened the sliding door and turned on the light for the big room, then stood there looking in, looking at all the fragments of old sets, at the wooden floor and stone walls.

Why here?

The other magical places he had heard of all had distinctive features to them—the standing stones at Stonehenge, the pyramids of Egypt, whatever. Was this new mystic power source just going to have a ramshackle little theater?

A theater with a mysterious pit under the basement? Maybe *that* was responsible for all this.

But really, it was just a theater.

It had been a church once, but it was a theater now.

He looked around at the stone walls with new insight. He had always known the building had its history, its idiosyncrasies, but he had always just accepted them. Now, for the first time, it occurred to him that the theater could be seen as a mysterious place, a magical place, quite aside from the plays performed there, and aside from the special, personal magic it had always held for him. Stone walls over a century old, an inexplicable and unexplored hole beneath it, a history that blended the sacred and the profane . . .

A few days ago, he knew he would have dismissed all that as nonsense, but now he wasn't sure.

If he refused to join the Bringers in their ritual, if he let magic die out completely, would the theater still have that special magical quality, when he was here alone? Was that actually magic? Was it inherent in the theater, a trace of its magical potential? Or was it just in *him*, just a matter of psychology, something that had nothing to do with *real* magic and wouldn't be changed?

A few days ago, he would have chosen the last without a moment's hesitation.

Now, though—even if it *was* just psychological, even if no true magic was involved, what would he think if he let the Bringers fail, and eleven of them actually did die? Could this place still be magical for him?

Somehow, he didn't think so.

He frowned. Did they have to die, then, if he didn't help?

The answer to that depended on several other questions. Had Maggie lied? If she had said what she believed to be true, was it *in fact* true, or had she been misled?

And was his choice really a simple either/or, between eleven deaths and unleashing wild new magic on the world?

Whatever the truth, he wanted to think it over and decide for himself, without getting anyone else involved yet; even if he couldn't settle the big questions, he could settle that. He really didn't need to add any more complications, as it was all quite complicated enough.

And that, he decided, meant that he wouldn't be calling Arnie Wechsler, or any other locksmith, in the morning; he wasn't ready to find out what was behind that other door. If his father asked, he'd say that the door had turned out to be just a closet.

Maybe, when he was a bit more confident that he understood what was going on, he could get a locksmith out here and see what was in there, but there wasn't any hurry. He really needed to think through what he had already learned. Whatever was behind the other door—Faerie or something else—was far more likely to provide more problems than to show him any solutions.

So it could wait. Everything down here could wait while he thought it all through.

He closed the sliding door and went upstairs.

He was sitting on the edge of the stage, still thinking, when the Bringers arrived.

That night he saw the play through, beginning to end,

as the Bringers rehearsed. He saw them working their spells, warming up, practicing for the big night, when the moon and stars would be right, when they would have an audience, when they would have to perform the entire thing nonstop, without break or flaw.

Afterward he talked to Maggie, and to Myrddin, whom he had known as Merle Innisfree.

Everything Maggie had told him in the fields of Faerie was confirmed; if he did not participate, the ritual would fail. Magic would pass from the world forever, and all the magicians but Maggie would die.

"There's no chance you could do it again in November?" he asked.

Myrddin and Maggie looked at one another. Then Myrddin shook his head.

"I shouldn't think so," he said. "I doubt there would be enough left of Sedona to serve our needs. And it wouldn't matter, in a way—you'd just be putting it off. Lad, you'd still know about it. We'd still need your help— but instead of here, it might be in Antarctica, or Kathmandu, or the Amazon jungles."

"Oh," Art said.

"We need you, Art," Maggie said. "Maybe I shouldn't have told you, but I didn't know what else to do."

"But turning magic loose—you say yourself you don't know what it'll do."

"It's been done before, you know," Myrddin pointed out. "The species seems to have survived."

"Are you sure? When was the last one of these . . . these things created? How do I know it wasn't magic that killed off the dinosaurs?"

Maggie looked startled; Myrddin said judiciously, "It might have been, at that, I suppose. And I've heard stories about Atlantis, of course. But Arthur, my lad, the Stonehenge power spot was only opened about eight thousand years ago, and Sedona probably a little after—though we don't know who started Sedona, or how, or why."

"Eight thousand years."

"About that."

"This hasn't been done in eight thousand years?"

Neither of them answered that.

"That's prehistoric. I mean, literally."

Myrddin nodded.

"You said you needed my participation," Art said.

"That's right," Myrddin replied.

"Participation, how?" Art asked. "The play's got seven roles, and the rest of you are mostly just a chorus—would I be in the chorus?"

"I suppose so, yes," Maggie said, with a glance at Myrddin. "I was sort of a late addition, and that's where I am."

"But I can't sing," Art protested. "I can't do magic. I don't act, you know, I never have—I don't think I'd remember my lines."

Maggie glanced worriedly at Myrddin, who smiled.

"Stage fright, lad? No need for that. You need to participate, true, but nobody said you had to *perform*."

Art needed a second to think about that; then he turned and looked at the neatly shelved lighting instruments.

"I expect it'll make the show look a little more professional, don't you?" Myrddin asked, putting an arm around Art's shoulders.

Chapter Seventeen

THE TEMPTATION to tell Marilyn when they met in Dumfrey's Antiques the next day was almost irresistible. The knowledge that she wouldn't believe him helped considerably in fighting temptation, but then came the realization that he could *prove* it to her by taking her down to the door into Faerie.

And that would also prove that he wasn't going insane, wasn't imagining the whole thing. He didn't really think he was deluded, but independent confirmation certainly wouldn't hurt his self-confidence.

That thought gnawed away at his resolve, and he almost cracked at lunch, when Marilyn asked if he'd figured out what the people who had rented the theater were up to.

But if he told her, she would have to join the show. She might not mind—or she might.

And what if he decided against participating, and she *didn't*?

She might blame him for eleven murders. She might blame him for wiping away the little magic that was left in the world—if that made any difference. Nobody knew if it made any difference, if anyone but the magicians would notice when it was gone.

And she might tell others, and each new person would mean a whole new debate.

"Oh," he said at last, "they're just doing a play, same as they said all along."

"Really?" Marilyn cocked her head. "But you said they weren't doing any preparation."

"Well, they weren't, but they are now. Got a slow start, that's all. I'll be hanging the lights tonight—or at least starting to."

Marilyn nodded. "So did you ever find out anything about this, what was it, 'mystic classic of the stage'?"

He nodded. "Yup. Turns out it was written by some secret society back around the turn of the century, or something, so it's always stayed sort of underground, never gotten wide distribution."

"Oh, foo, that's no fun, then! That takes almost all the mystery out of it!" She slapped at him gently.

"Sorry," he said, smiling.

"I mean, what good are a bunch of mysterious strangers if they aren't smuggling dope or something?"

"Not much," he agreed, suppressing a grin.

"So are they planning to advertise this show of theirs? I haven't seen any posters or anything."

Art shrugged. "I don't know," he said. "Hey, have you seen Susan around lately?"

The conversation wandered away from the theater, but Marilyn's question lingered, and that night, as he pulled the first Fresnel off the shelf, Art asked Myrddin, "Do you guys want an audience for this thing?"

"Why do you ask?"

Art shrugged, and one of the shutters on the lighting instrument rattled. "Just curious," he said.

"Well, as it happens, we *need* an audience—and we expect to have one," Myrddin told him.

"Really? You haven't done any advertising, have you?"

Myrddin grinned at him. "I never said the audience would be *human*," he replied.

Art decided not to ask any more questions just yet.

He couldn't stop thinking about it, though, as he clamped the lighting instruments in place.

He had decided on a simple design that would reflect the mystic circles that made up much of the play; a ring of Fresnels gelled warm gold and pale pink would flood the center of the stage with light, and an outer ring of licos gelled medium blue would provide background and accent. Specials were set for each upstage corner, for the scenes when characters popped up there unexpectedly. The downstage corners and the outer edges were left dark—they weren't used, and he didn't have the equipment to spare for them.

Never said the audience would be human, Myrddin had said. Art looked down from the catwalk at the Bringers in their places, running through the dialogue. They had never said the audience would be human, but there they were, going through their paces, untroubled by it. He looked at their shadows on the stage and remembered his business.

Real strip lights would have been nice, but the theater didn't have them and he'd never gotten around to making any. If he got lucky, and didn't need a week just to eliminate unwanted shadows, he might still have time to do something about that. For now, though, he expected he would have to resort to the same trick he'd been using for the past ten years, taping unframed gels over the onstage work lights and cutting a dimmer into the circuit.

If not human, then what? What else was there? As he climbed down the stage-left ladder a flare of enchanted flame lit the wall around him, which was no comfort at all.

Back at the equipment shelves he counted the Fresnels. He would have one left over; now, where could he put that to do the most good? He looked out at the stage as the magicians stepped back in simulated surprise at the High Mage's anger.

Myrddin hadn't meant magicians; all the magicians in the world were in the show, not the audience, and besides, they seemed human enough, generally speaking.

They didn't really have a curtain-warmer; that should properly take at least three instruments, and he wasn't going to have any leftover licos, not after he rigged the specials for the corners, but a lone Fresnel with the shutters wide open would be better than nothing, especially if he angled it across. He'd need to think about which side to put it on; the show was just about the most symmetrical he'd ever lit, which didn't help. He slipped out onto the downstage corner to look the situation over, carefully avoiding Baba Yeager as she made her exit.

Here he could look out over the empty house, and wonder what would be in those chairs. Not magicians—what else, then? Magical beings of some sort?

He forced himself back to business. If he hung the Fresnel at stage left, it would partially light the steps at stage right; if he hung it stage right, they'd be in complete darkness. The show didn't use the steps, so ordinarily he wouldn't want to call the audience's attention to them, but this wasn't ordinary. He looked out at the house again.

He didn't know what the audience would *be*. Gods? Demons? Fairies? Elves? Gryphons, dragons, unicorns? Would they care about the steps? Would the cast want to be able to see the steps in case something went wrong?

Elves, fairies—and there was a door to Faerie downstairs. Was *that* where the audience would come from? He looked out into the darkness and tried to imagine elves sitting out there.

Hang it at stage right, he decided. Whatever the audience was, he thought he'd be happier emphasizing their separation from the events onstage.

Separation—an idea stirred somewhere in the back of his mind as he went to the shelves and lifted down the instrument he wanted.

He stood for a long moment with the Fresnel in his hand, looking up at the iron lighting frame mounted to the right side of the proscenium, but the idea wouldn't come clear. Instead, a question came to him.

Why was he doing this?

Why was he hanging these lights when he hadn't yet decided whether he wanted to help out?

If he refused to go along, would they cancel the show, or would they try it without him?

Would just having hung the lights be enough cooperation?

Did he really want to unleash wild new magic on an unsuspecting world? As before, a surge of terror hit him at the thought—and something else underneath it.

Real magic.

Kier Kaye muffed a line and burst out laughing; Yeager called a rude comment, and Dr. Torralva gently reprimanded them both.

They didn't seem worried by the prospect of dying before the year was out—but then, they expected the ritual to work.

Could they be so sure, though? Shouldn't they be more worried than this?

Yeager was still in the stage-left wings; she wouldn't

reenter the action for a few minutes yet. With the Fresnel still in his hand, Art ambled over to talk to her.

"Go away, boy," she told him.

"Ms. Yeager," he began.

"Pah!" she snapped, followed by something in a language he didn't understand. It sounded like Russian. It also sounded insulting. "If you *must* talk to me," she said, reverting to English, "at least use my right name, now that you know who we are, and not that stupid lie they made up for me. It's Yaga, not Yeager—I'm no damned German!"

"I'm sorry," he said.

"You should be."

"I wanted to ask, though . . ."

"Then ask."

"About this . . . this performance. What if it doesn't work?"

She turned and stared at him, with yellowed and terrifying eyes. After a moment of silence, a moment in which Myrddin's onstage dialogue could be clearly heard, she snorted.

"If it doesn't work," she said, "the world will be a sad, drab place, and I won't much mind missing it."

"Missing it?"

"Well, I'll be dead and gone, won't I, chick? We all will. By Christmas. They told you that, I'm sure—even if that little ninny who calls herself a witch forgot, Myrddin wouldn't miss a chance."

"You're sure?"

"Are you questioning me?"

"Oh, no!" Art protested. "Nothing like that!"

"Well, then."

"When you say the world will be sad . . . how do you mean that? What will change, really?"

Again, she took her time about replying.

"Having second thoughts, are you?" she demanded at last.

Art didn't answer; he didn't even try.

118

"Well, I'll tell you, I don't know what it'll be like, really, any more than the rest of 'em. I don't suppose it'll be as different as all that—but who knows? You can't use magic to see a world where magic isn't possible. I suppose you people will go on just as you have these last few centuries. You probably won't even miss it." She grinned, revealing hideous teeth, yellow and sharp. "Or maybe you'll all drop dead, or turn to apes—maybe your minds are all magical. Who knows?"

Art hesitated, trying to think what to ask next, while the old woman was in a reasonably talkative mood, but just then her cue came, and she turned away, returning to the stage.

Art stood for a long moment, holding the Fresnel, then headed out to hang it.

Chapter Eighteen

FOUR DAYS later, on Friday, Art had the lights hung, aimed, gelled, and shuttered, and he had still not decided whether to go through with the ritual.

He had argued with Marilyn without really knowing why, and had left her on the verge of tears with no clear understanding of what she was upset about.

He had, however, retrieved the idea that had come to him.

The Bringers were supposedly doomed to die because the world would no longer have any magic in it—so why not find them another world?

If they all went through that door in the basement, stepped through into Faerie, and just stayed there when the door disappeared, wouldn't they be safe enough? Faerie wasn't going to vanish when the magic from Arizona died; Faerie *must* still have magic. How else could it be Faerie?

And the normal, everyday world would still be intact, without any wild magic turned loose. Bampton would still be a quiet little suburb. Art's life could continue undisturbed, and there wouldn't be any worries about New England becoming the next Atlantis.

He wished he had come up with this when he had still been working on focusing lights, using various members of the group as lighting dummies—that would have made conversation convenient and natural. Right at the moment, the Bringers were onstage discussing something among themselves—he couldn't hear what, and although he was now allowed to watch rehearsals, and was accepted as a necessary part of the performance, he was still not a full member of the group.

Not that he particularly wanted to be. He was a techie, not a magician.

Well, sometime soon he and the director would need to sit down together and go over the lighting cues, and he could bring up his idea then.

"Arthur!" Myrddin called, almost as if he had heard Art's thought. Art looked up from the lighting board, startled. "Arthur, lad, come here a moment, would you?"

Puzzled, Art came.

"We've been talking it over, the lot of us," Myrddin explained. "We've been looking at the lights you've got up there, and we were thinking that it might be nice if we had some *sets*, as well—I mean, if we're really going to do this up as a play, and not just use that as an excuse, we might as well get it right, eh?"

"But it *is* a play . . ."

"Well, I wrote it that way, but that was so we wouldn't have any trouble over it. I wrote it up as a church service, too—if we'd come out with a place where there was a church available instead of a theater, we'd be doing *that* version."

"Really?"

"Really. I wrote it half a dozen ways. Now, what do you think about some sets?"

"Well, but, I mean, the sets are all supposed to be in place before the lights go up—I'll have to refocus everything."

"Will you?"

"Yes!"

Myrddin looked up at the lights, then back at Art. "Well, that'll give you something to do for the next two weeks, then, won't it?"

Art's mouth opened, then snapped shut.

So much for building proper strips. Maybe he could do that this winter, if there wasn't enough snow to keep him busy.

"Anyway," Myrddin went on, "we wanted to ask your advice. We don't need new sets—Maggie tells us you have old ones in the cellars, same as you have those over there." He pointed at the leftovers from *Midsummer Night's Dream*, which still hadn't been moved to the basement.

"Well, yeah," Art admitted.

"Splendid! We'll just take a look at them, then, and choose the ones we want . . ."

"Mr. Innisfree," Art interrupted desperately, "you don't need to do that."

"Ah, but we want to, lad! Add a bit of your stage magic to our own, we will—and all the better for making *new* magic, I'm sure!"

"You don't need new magic, though."

Myrddin stopped his speech abruptly and stared at Art; so did several of the others.

"What you say there, child?" Tituba Smith demanded.

"Art, that's the whole *point*," Maggie called.

"New magic for old, new magic for old!" Granny Yaga chanted, parrotlike, before bursting out in a raucous cackle.

"But you don't," Art insisted. "If the world loses its magic, you can all still go live in Faerie."

121

Myrddin blinked solemnly at Art.

"And how are we supposed to get to Faerie?" Morgan asked, her hands on her hips.

"Through the door in the basement," Art replied, startled by the question.

Morgan glared, first at Art, then around at the others. "Is this true?" she demanded. "Nobody told *me* about any door in the basement!"

"We didn't?" Maggie said, as startled as Art had been.

"Morgan," Myrddin said, a hand raised in a calming gesture, "I'm sorry, I admit it, that was my doing. I didn't trust you—you know why. I feared if you knew of the door that you'd leave us, and I don't know if we could succeed without you at this point."

Morgan glowered at him, and Myrddin faced up to it.

"I'll not flee to the Other Realm," Rabbitt announced. "This world is my own, and I'll live or die in it."

Several voices murmured, and worried eyes turned toward Morgan.

"Oh, I'll stay," Morgan said, "until the spell is cast; then I'll go back where I belong, where I should have been these past two centuries."

"I'd prefer Earth, if I have a choice," Kaye remarked, "but if anything goes wrong, I'd prefer Faerie to death."

"What's it like in Faerie, now?" Karagöz asked. "Who did you see?"

"No one," Maggie said. "Just an empty meadow."

An uneasy silence followed this, broken a moment later when Tituba asked, "You didn't see *no one*? Not even off in the distance?"

"I thought I saw towers," Art said. "Beyond the trees. And there were birds. And butterflies."

"In all my years, I've never heard of anyone entering Faerie without encountering its inhabitants," said Tanner.

"Maybe it is dead," Wang suggested. "Maybe *their* magic ran out even before ours."

That possibility had not occurred to Art.

"But the door . . ." he began.

"The door is in *our* world," Rabbitt pointed out, "conjured by the spells we've begun here."

Art stared at the magicians. His great idea had not resolved his dilemma; instead it had created even more questions.

"We'll have to explore," Morgan said. When several voices started to protest, she raised a stilling hand and added, "Once the ritual is done, that is."

"And if the spell fails, perhaps we can slip through before the door fades, as the young man suggested," Wang pointed out. "That would surely be preferable to certain death."

That evoked a general chorus of agreement—but Art noticed that Myrddin and a couple of the others didn't join in. He stared at them all hopelessly.

Maybe he had found them a way out—but maybe he hadn't.

And that meant he still didn't know what to do, whether to help them unleash chaos, or to refuse and see what happened.

At least he'd reduced it from eleven murders to a mere gamble with eleven lives. He sighed. He'd tried—and they'd chosen to take the risks.

At that point Myrddin decided the time had come to drag the conversation back to its original track. He said, "Now, about those sets . . ."

Chapter Nineteen

THE STAGE was a phantasmagorical clutter of mismatched elements, but that didn't seem to trouble any of the Bringers of Wonder at all. A castle wall loomed in the upstage right corner, a flowering hedge upstage left, with an art deco triumphal arch, originally intended for a nightclub

set, between them. The chalk circles had been redrawn on
a sloping platform originally built for a production of *The
Roar of the Greasepaint* that had been one of the first
shows Art had worked on. Roman columns adorned either
side of the stage, alternating with Victorian streetlamps,
the entire array supporting a glittering mesh, draped in
graceful swags in two long arcs, one on either side.

The whole effect was supremely weird—not mystical so
much as just plain strange. It resembled an architectural
warehouse more than a wizard's laboratory.

For two weeks, Art had been desperately reworking his
lighting to suit this new, cluttered stage, and all the while,
as he worked, he was trying to decide, trying to think—
and trying *not* to think.

He had not gone near the mysterious black door in the
basement again, but some of the others had—Karagöz,
Tanner, and Kaye had ventured in, in a cautious little
group. Morgan had not accompanied them; everyone
agreed that she knew Faerie better than anyone on Earth,
but she had declined the invitation to join the exploratory
party. She preferred not to risk the temptation she knew
she would feel to stay in the Twilight Lands.

Upon their return the explorers reported that magic still
worked in Faerie—but differently. They couldn't explain
that. And they hadn't yet met any of the inhabitants. Due
to the time differential between Earth and Faerie they had
not dared venture far, lest they miss the performance—
everyone knew that an hour or two in Faerie might easily
turn into days or weeks back on Earth.

That left more mysteries, made every guess about the
future more difficult.

And other manifestations of the supernatural had arisen
to keep Art's attention divided. Something was definitely
alive in the pit beneath the basement, for one thing; Art
could hear it snuffling and slithering about. Sometimes it
thumped against the wooden floor.

It didn't seem particularly annoyed or dangerous,

though, and the thumps sounded more like random explorations than an attempt to break out. Art had told the others about it; no one had any idea what it was, and after much debate they had resolved to leave it alone.

As well, there were small glowing things that drifted about in the basement sometimes. Nobody had gotten a good look at one. They came in three colors, red, green, and gold.

And they were beautiful. Art often glimpsed them from a distance, or from the corner of his eye, or vanishing around a doorway, and every time he stopped and stared, and every time they were gone before he could see more than a vague impression of colored light, of something small and delicate and graceful moving through the air, glowing brightly.

Art thought they might be fairies—after all, if the land beyond the door was Faerie, why not? Not the lordly fey folk of *A Midsummer Night's Dream*, of course, but little winged creatures, the sort in Victorian children's books, or Disney's *Fantasia*. Why not?

The Bringers just shrugged; they didn't know what the lights were, either. This didn't trouble them; they *expected* new magic to be different from anything they'd known.

Art couldn't get a good look at the things, couldn't tell if they were fairies, or some sort of mutant firefly, or something else entirely. He felt as if he ought to be frightened by such things, but he wasn't.

Fear came from threats, after all, from danger—or from the unknown. But the little glowing things posed no threat that he could see, and the Bringers assured him that whatever they were, they weren't dangerous.

And they weren't really unknown. They were *magic*. Raw magic, bubbling over, spilling back in time, shapeless and random—and harmless.

It was very odd, just how certain Art was that the lights were harmless. Sometimes that certainty troubled him slightly, but he was so sure he was right, what harm could it do that he didn't know *why* he was sure?

And they were a distraction. He didn't have time to worry about Faerie or the thing in the pit or the drifting lights, or the bone-handled dagger or the box of treasures or the locked door in the wardrobe room. He had lights to aim, cues to learn, and a vital decision to make.

Would he go through with the performance?

On Monday of the final week, Marilyn knocked at the stage door around midnight to suggest a late-night snack together. He was distracted, not thinking, and let her in while he locked up.

The Bringers had departed a few minutes before, so it seemed safe enough. He left her staring at the muddle of sets while he checked the basement doors.

He wished he could have locked the door to Faerie, but none of the keys would fit.

As he was climbing the stairs again a flight of the glowing things cruised past him, vanishing around a corner under the steps. He paid no attention until he looked up and saw Marilyn standing in the open doorway, staring.

"What were *those*?" she asked.

He glanced down just in time to see the glow fade; as usual, he hadn't gotten a clear look at them.

"Fireflies," he said.

"I never saw fireflies like that," Marilyn said. "Besides, it's too late in the year, isn't it? And how'd they get in here?"

"Well, I don't know, then," he said, shrugging.

Marilyn stared at him, then down at the point where the lights had vanished.

"I don't know," Art repeated defensively.

"Okay," Marilyn said, "I'm not arguing; you coming?"

The date was not a success; Marilyn made no further mention of the mysterious elfin lights, but somehow, after she had marveled at the bizarre stage set and Art had mumbled unresponsively in return, they wound up first discussing, and then arguing about, Maggie Gowdie. Marilyn managed to take offense at Art's passing mention that Maggie's grandmother had claimed to be a Scottish witch.

Art's heart wasn't in the argument, though; he was always thinking, underneath, about the big question.

Should he go through with his part of the performance?

Wednesday Jamie came back from California, broke and tanned and full of stories about L.A.—and curious about what was happening at the theater.

"A play," Art told him.

"What kind of play?"

Art couldn't answer that; his thoughts on the subject were too confused.

"You'll have to come see it," he said.

Instantly he regretted it. Hadn't Myrddin said the audience wasn't to be human?

He didn't want to say any more, and did his best to steer the conversation back to Hollywood, where he could safely ignore it while he thought about his choices.

Then it was Saturday, and the point of no return was nearing. He had gone through lighting rehearsal, full tech rehearsal, dress rehearsal, without voicing his indecision, without saying anything to disturb the Bringers' calm assurance that he would cooperate. And the performance was to be this evening.

If he was going to back out, he had to do it *now*, while there was time for the Bringers to flee into Faerie—those who preferred escape to death, at any rate. He guessed that would be roughly an even split.

He stood by his lighting board, checking how the blue wash at the edge looked on Rabbitt's skin, and trying to make up his mind about two things at once: Should he do a last-minute gel change? Did he *want* to unleash magic on the world?

In the blue light Rabbitt looked even darker than he ordinarily did, but it was a healthy enough color; Art thought it would do.

No new gel, then.

But magic . . .

"Mr. Rabbitt," he asked, "what'll it be like?"

He had hinted at the question repeatedly, had even asked it directly, and had never gotten a good answer; he was making one last try.

The huge magician cocked his head in Art's direction. "Do you mean, when the magic is come?"

"Yeah."

Rabbitt smiled wryly. "In truth, lad, none of us really, entirely knows what will happen." He waved theatrically. "It might be that unicorns will be reborn, that dragons will walk the mountains once again—or perhaps not, perhaps the magic will take new and strange forms." He dropped his arm and shrugged. "Whatever unintended side effects we may achieve, we can be certain that magic will once again be so accessible that anyone with the will and belief will be able to use it, not just wizards and mages."

"Anyone?"

"Oh, nearly."

"Well, I mean . . . who?"

"You, perhaps." He smiled again. "It's said that young lovers will be particularly good at it. That's if the stories are to be trusted, of course."

"I'm not a young lover," Art protested.

"Ah," Rabbitt said, with a broad grin, "but perhaps you *will* be."

Art frowned.

Something bright and green flitted across the periphery of his vision; he started and stared.

One of the mysterious lights from the basement, the fairies or will-o'-the-wisps or whatever they were, had ventured up the stairs and emerged onto the stage.

This was the first time one of the more obviously magical spontaneous phenomena, as opposed to the Bringers' spells, had manifested itself anywhere except the basement.

And it didn't vanish when he stared at it; it flickered,

and darted about so that he couldn't see it clearly, but it didn't vanish.

He looked at his watch. Less than an hour before curtain.

He had to decide.

"Art?" someone called.

He turned and found Maggie beside him, and was oddly disappointed.

"Hi," she said. "Hope I didn't startle you."

"Just pre-show jitters," he said.

"Yeah," she replied, forcing a smile, "me, too. But anyway, I need the key to the box office."

He blinked at her. "You do?" he asked stupidly.

"Well, yes, of course I do," she said. "I'm manning the booth."

He stared at her, uncomprehending.

"Selling tickets," she explained. "Someone has to. People are coming to see the show, you know. Even though we didn't advertise except the one poster out front."

"They are?"

"Sure. A lot of your friends from *Dream*, for one thing—they're all curious about us."

"You have tickets?"

"Conjured them myself—with ten bucks at the local print shop." Grinning, she held up a stack of printed red pasteboard. "The key?"

"Uh." He reached in his pocket, then stopped. "I'll take care of it," he said. "Someone needs to open the doors, too, right?"

She asked, "You don't need to be back here?"

"Not right now."

Together they walked up the aisle, and he stared out at the empty seats.

Somehow, he had become so involved with the ritual aspect of the play he had forgotten that it was a *play*, a performance people could watch and enjoy even if they didn't know about spells or magic or other mysteries.

But it was a play, and there would be an audience, with real, everyday people in it.

In the lobby he unlocked the box office without a word, then crossed to the big front doors. He threw back the bolt and opened the right-hand door an inch or two, then peered out the crack.

Marilyn and Jamie were already waiting on the sidewalk, talking idly. They were standing apart; Marilyn's hands were behind her, against a signpost, while Jamie's were in the pockets of his cutoff jeans. They weren't looking at him.

They were here to see the show.

At that moment, Art suddenly knew what he had to do.

It didn't matter if it changed everything. It didn't matter if it was dangerous—after all, what was life without a little risk? What was life without a little magic? He'd invited Jamie here himself. He couldn't disappoint an audience.

After all, magic or no magic—the show must go on.

Chapter Twenty

ONLY ABOUT thirty citizens of Bampton were in the audience, yet when Art risked a glance around the curtain in the middle of the first act he saw no empty seats.

Just what was occupying the others he couldn't really say. Some of them had faces, some didn't. There were the mysterious cellar lights flitting here and there, too. And he could hear something thumping under the stage.

The Bringers of Wonder were untroubled by such details as they went through their performance.

Art had seen real magic in it before, in rehearsals, but nothing like what he saw now. Strange colors flickered in every corner; magic swirled in the air, surged back and forth in waves. He could feel it, like an impending thunderstorm, but a thousand times more intense.

He wondered what the humans in the audience made of it.

Then he heard his next cue coming, and he slipped back to the lighting board, and back to his work.

There was no intermission between acts; Art could feel himself that the magic wouldn't allow it. It had waited, somewhere, for a very long time; now it was awake and eager, not to be held back.

The second act was brief and simple: in it the mage and his apprentices confronted the gods and demanded that magic be restored to the world; the gods considered the request, and then granted it, expelling the dragon that had kept magic confined—or perhaps instead freeing the dragon that was magic itself; the play was deliberately ambiguous.

In rehearsal, Al Tanner, playing the gods' spokesman, had provided an illusion of a dragon for the climax, when the dragon burst forth from its cave; Art had considered it a rather unconvincing illusion and a weak ending.

As he felt the magical forces crawling across his skin and flashing through him, as he saw the light from his instruments bend and twist and change, he began to wonder whether Tanner's illusion would work properly.

And as the final scene began, Tanner did not raise his wand. The thumping from beneath the stage sounded again, louder than before. Art felt a sudden surge of panic.

By then it was too late to do anything; the floor burst open in a spectacular roaring explosion of flame and splinters, and the Dragon arose, spreading its wings.

Shining emerald green, wings lined with black and with colors Art could not name, the Dragon rose from the crypts beneath the stage and looked out at the audience with blazing eyes. The Bringers of Wonder tumbled back away from the monster, which seemed to fill the entire stage; the mismatched sets toppled and shattered, falling in fiberboard and plaster ruin. Art wanted to run away, to flee in terror; he wanted to run out onstage and do something to the Dragon, anything, to make it go away. He wanted to jump down into the audience and protect Marilyn.

What he actually did, though, was to bring up the center-stage ring of licos to full, and keep the blue background lights at half while dropping everything else to black. The Dragon was lit in a blaze of glory, the golden light glittering from its vivid green scales.

Cue 49. Myrddin had insisted on it, even though Art had said it wouldn't look right on Tanner's illusion.

Myrddin had been right.

Then the Dragon rose up out of the stage and vanished into the flies overhead, and Art looked up, astonished.

He saw only the catwalk and the lights and the ropes and the other normal overhead clutter. The Dragon was gone.

It was gone—but where?

Then he smiled, remembering. Illusion. The essence of magic is deceit. There was no dragon, really; Tanner had just done a better job with his tricks.

Then he looked out at the stage.

The lights were wrong; he'd missed his cue. Quickly, he went to Cue 50, and brought up #7 while slowly fading everything else.

Myrddin was out of position, knocked aside by the great beast—or by Tanner's illusion, whichever it was. Now he scrambled across the stage to take his place under the spotlight for his closing speech.

Art watched, and saw him stumble as his foot came down on a board that gave beneath him; the floorboard had been broken by the dragon.

Then the magician was standing in his place in the light, declaiming his lines, and Maggie was hauling on the curtain, Dr. Torralva helping her. Myrddin spoke his final line, Art brought down #7 in a three-beat fade, and the curtain swung closed.

Applause swelled up from the audience, invisible beyond the closed curtain.

The show was over.

There were to be no curtain calls; in fact, Art realized as he brought up the curtain-warmer that several of the Bringers seemed to have vanished. None of the onstage or backstage lights were on, but an eerie glow seemed to suffuse everything; by it Art could see Maggie and Myrddin and Morgan and Dr. Torralva, and a fox was standing atop the stump of a papier-mâché streetlamp, but the others were gone.

Had the Dragon gotten them, eaten them, consumed them somehow?

But the Dragon wasn't real . . .

But then what had wrecked the stage?

And had the ceremony worked? Myrddin and Morgan and Torralva were still alive, but what about the others? Maybe the whole thing had been a bust, and the others had died, had turned to dust and blown away.

No. He knew that wasn't what had happened. He could feel the magic in the air, could feel it pouring up out of the hole in the stage, like cool air from a cave, like the electric tingle of static, like the heat from a furnace, all at once—and not really like any of them. The spell had worked.

In fact, he could almost *see* the magic bubbling and spilling out of the hole, in blue and purple and colors he had never seen or imagined before, like heat shimmer and sparks.

He really, really hoped that hole was an illusion, or just the traps opened.

But he still had something more immediate to worry about. The applause had become ragged and uncertain, but there was still an audience out there.

The show must go on. He had his job to do.

He brought down the curtain-warmer, waited a long five beats, and brought up the houselights. That should make it plain that the show was over.

Sure enough, the applause died away during the five beats of darkness, and was gone by the time the house-lights were up full.

His job was done.

The show was over, and magic was loose upon the world—in theory. Whatever that really meant.

He couldn't resist; he left the board, crossed to the curtain, and peeped out around the end.

The audience was beginning to drift out to the lobby.

Somehow, despite the feel of raw magical energy in the air, Art had assumed that when the play was done the various mysterious phenomena would cease, and the supernatural portion of the audience would vanish.

They had done nothing of the sort.

There were goblins bouncing on the cushions in several seats; translucent things that Art took for ghosts were floating up and down the aisles. The ordinary citizens of Bampton were all out in the lobby—the few faces Art could glimpse at that distance, through the doors, looked apprehensive.

All but one, that is. Marilyn was standing at the foot of the stage. She spotted him peering out, and waved.

He waved back, took a quick glance at the ruins, at the remaining magicians, and beckoned to her.

She hopped quickly up onto the stage and slipped around the end of the curtain.

"Art," she said, "that was incredible."

"Yeah," Art agreed. He took a final glance out at the house, then stepped back to the board and turned on the work lights. He caught Marilyn's hand, and together they looked at the damage.

The sets were shattered and scattered; bits of painted paper and wood were everywhere. Some of them were scorched and blackened.

And the stage was smashed open. There could be no doubt; it had *not* been an illusion.

Cautiously, the two of them advanced to the edge, not speaking, stepping carefully, testing each board before putting weight on it. When they neared the edge, Art leaned forward and peered down into the hole.

He could see the big basement room, the unused old sets, the stone walls, all lit by an eldritch red glow. The center of the wooden floor was gone, however, and he could also see down into the pit beneath, the pit that went down deep into the living stone beneath the theater.

That was where the glow seemed to be coming from.

All that should be down there, he knew, was old trash, but that was not what he saw.

Instead, he saw the Dragon, looking up at him, red eyes glowing in its shadowed face.

It was unquestionably the same dragon. There couldn't be two like that.

"But it vanished going *up*," Marilyn protested. "How could it be back down there?"

"Magic," Art said.

"It *is* magic, isn't it?" Marilyn said. "Those things in the audience—they aren't just midgets in costume, or special effects, are they?"

"Is that what you thought?" Art asked, startled. He had become so accustomed to magic over the past three weeks that he had forgotten how this must all seem to Marilyn.

She didn't answer. He sighed, and said, "I guess I'd better explain."

"About time," she told him.

By the time he finished telling her everything they were sitting on the porch steps outside the stage door and dawn was breaking in the east. Myrddin had interrupted them once to apologize. The old magician had then used his magic to repair the stage and clear away the destroyed sets and props—even *he* had been surprised by how easy the spell was—while Marilyn stared in wonder.

After that, any question she might have had about the reality of magic was gone, gone as completely as the hole in the floor.

When the repairs were done, Myrddin had departed.

All the Bringers of Wonder had departed. Art wasn't

sure how or where, or whether they might return, but they were definitely gone.

The magic spilling from the theater washed over Art and Marilyn like a warm summer rain as they sat and talked. When Art tried, he could see it rolling out across the parking lot, climbing the lampposts on Thoreau Street, spreading across the sky overhead.

Marilyn had not had a month of practice to become sensitized to it, but she, too, could feel it, and she had seen the play, had seen Myrddin at work afterward. When Art had finished his explanation she had no doubt of its truth.

Sunlight streaked overhead, tangling with the magic; for a moment, invisible colors spilled from the air. Marilyn and Art sat side by side on the steps, thinking, feeling the eerie new world, looking out at the transformed and familiar reality of Bampton.

Old Spanner was out in his field, but Marilyn noticed something different about him. She pointed.

"Look," she said.

Art looked, as Spanner spread wide fine new wings. He flexed great white feathers and took to the air. As the two watched, the old horse sailed upward, sunlight gleaming from his flanks, tail flying in the breeze.

Tiny humanoid creatures, naked and shining, fluttered down from the theater eaves on dragonfly wings, to circle Art's head and then dance away through the air.

"What are they?" Marilyn asked. "Fairies?"

"Who knows?" Art asked. "Sprites, elves, fairies—I don't know the distinctions." He got to his feet and helped Marilyn up.

"We'll have to learn them," Marilyn said.

"Or make them up," Art replied. "These might be new, not the old things at all." He grinned, and waved a hand, painting a polychrome glimmer in the air.

Together they walked across the parking lot, hand in hand, trailing rainbows, as gnomes peered from the mailbox on the corner, elves danced on the sidewalk, and the morning sun smiled down at them all.

Somewhere overhead, Spanner sang as his wings caught the jeweled breeze.

THE FINAL FOLLY
OF CAPTAIN DANCY

1.

I was right there beside him when it happened, and I saw the whole thing. It wasn't anything but pure bad luck, such as could happen to anyone—but it had never happened to the captain before, and I'd guess he wasn't ready for it.

We had just come out of Old Joe's Tavern, where the captain had beaten the snot out of three young troublemakers, and we'd left by way of the alley, since the troublemakers had shipmates of their own, and that alleyway wasn't any too clean. I didn't see exactly what it was the captain stepped in, but it was brown and greasy, and when his foot hit it that foot went straight out from under him and he fell, and his head fetched up hard against the brick wall, and there was a snap like kindling broken across your knee, and there he was on the ground, dead.

It was pure bad luck, and the damnedest thing, but that's how it happened, and Captain Jack Dancy, who'd had three ships shot out from under him, who'd come through the battle of Cushgar Corners, where only three men survived, without a scratch, who'd sired bastards on half the wives in Collyport without ever a husband suspecting, who'd stolen the entire treasury from the Pundit of Oul and got away clean, who'd escaped from the Dungeon Pits of the Black Sorcerer on Little Hengist, who was the only man ever pardoned by Governor "Hangman" Lee, who'd climbed Dawson's Butte with only a bullwhip for tackle—that man, Jolly Jack Dancy, lay dead in the alley behind Old Joe's Tavern of a simple fall and a broken neck.

And that meant that me and the rest of the crew of the good ship *Bonny Anne* were in deep trouble.

We didn't know the half of it yet, of course, but even then, drunk as I was, I knew it wasn't good.

I saw him fall, and I heard his neck break, but I was muddled by drink, and I didn't really believe that the captain could die like any other mortal, and most particularly not in such a stupid and easy fashion, so I judged that he was just hurt, and I picked him up and tried to get him to walk, but a corpse doesn't do much walking without at least a bit of a charm put on it, so then I swung him up across my shoulders and I headed down that alley, swaying slightly, and in a hurry to get back to the *Bonny Anne*, where either Doc Brewer or the captain's lady, Miss Melissa, could see about reviving him.

I think somewhere at the back of my mind I must have known he was dead, but sozzled as I was I probably thought even that wouldn't necessarily have been entirely permanent. I've seen my share of zombies, and I know they aren't of much use and don't remember a damned bit of what they knew in life, but I'd heard tales of other ways of dealing with the dead, one sort of necromancy or the other, and I won't call them lies as yet.

I had enough sense left to stay in the alleys as much as I could, and halfway to the docks I ran into Black Eddie driving a freight wagon, and I hailed him and threw the captain's carcass in the back, and then climbed up beside him.

It took me two or three tries to get up to the driver's bench, what with the liquor in me, but I made it eventually, and Black Eddie had us rolling before I had my ass on the plank.

"Head for the ship," I told him, and he nodded, as he was already bound that way. He snapped the reins and sped the horses a mite.

Then he threw a look behind him, and turned to me.

"Billy," he said, "What's wrong wi' the Captain?"

"Broke his fool neck," said I.

He looked at me startled, then looked back at that corpse, and then asked, "You mean he's dead?"

I started to nod, and then to shrug, and then I said, "Damned if I know, Eddie, but I'm afraid so."

"Damme!" Eddie said, and he flicked the reins again for more speed.

That brought our situation to my attention. "Eddie," said I, looking around in puzzlement, "What're ye doing with this wagon?"

"Damned if *I* know, Billy," he said. " 'Twas the captain's order that I get it, and have it at the docks by midnight, but he didn't think to tell me why."

"Oh," I said, trying to remember if the captain had said anything about a wagon, and not managing to recall much of anything at all. The captain had mostly been on about the usual, whiskey and women and the woes of the world, and hadn't spoken much of any special plans. A moment or two later we rolled out onto the dock where the *Bonny Anne* lay, and I hadn't come up with a thing.

"Well," I said, "Mr. Abernathy will know."

We'd tied up right to the dock, as the harbor in Collyport is a good and deep one, with a drop-off as steep as a ship-chandler's prices; no need to ride out at anchor and come in with the boats, as there would be in most of the ports we traded in. About a dozen ships were in port, at one place or another, and the *Bonny Anne* was one of them, right there at hand, and we could see the lads aboard her watching as we came riding up.

Looking up at them, the thought came to me that perhaps there were things we had best keep to ourselves, at least until we'd had a chance to talk matters over with our first mate, Lieutenant John Hastings Abernathy, who had the watch aboard and was Captain Dancy's closest confidant. It seemed to me I recalled a few things I hadn't before.

"Eddie," said I, "give me a hand with the captain, would you? And let on he's just drunk, or been clouted, and let's not say any more of it than we must, shall we?"

He gave me the fish-eye, but then he shrugged. "What the hell, then," he said. "Let it be Mr. Abernathy what spreads the news, if you like."

"It'd suit me," I said. I was thinking of a deal the Captain had made, six years before, with the Caliburn Witch.

So the two of us hauled that corpse out of the wagon with a bit more care than was honestly called for, and we got it upright between us, me with my hand at the back of the head so the crew would not be seeing it loll off to one side too badly, and we walked up the gangplank with the feet dragging between us, and we headed straight back to the captain's cabin.

Old Wheeler, the captain's man, was pottering about, and we shooed him away and dumped poor old Jack Dancy's mortal remains on the bunk, and then Black Eddie sent me to fetch Mr. Abernathy.

I found Hasty Bernie on the quarterdeck, just where he should have been, and had little doubt in my mind that he'd watched us every inch from the wagon to the break in the poop, but he didn't let on a bit, he just watched me walk up, and stood there silent as a taut sail until I said, "Permission to speak, sir?"

"Go ahead, Mr. Jones," he said, and I knew we were being formal, as he didn't call me Billy, but I didn't quite see why, as yet.

"Mr. Abernathy," I said, "I'd like a word with you in private, if I might, regardin' the captain."

He lifted up on his toes, with his hands behind his back, the way he always did when he was nervous about something, and he said, "And what is it that you can't say right here, Mr. Jones? Who's to hear you?"

I wasn't happy to hear that, at all. He must have thought I was getting out of line somehow, and I remembered as he'd asked me especially to keep a close eye on some of the men, as they might be thinking the captain wasn't looking out for them proper.

I wasn't too concerned about mutiny brewing, not just

then, in particular as I *had* been keeping an eye out, and hadn't seen a man aboard who didn't have faith in the captain. They might not think much of the rest of us, but they all admired the captain and trusted in him to do right by them.

Which made my news that much worse. "Mr. Abernathy," said I, "you know as well as I do that any word said on this deck can be heard by any as might care to listen from below the rail, either on the halfdeck or on the docks, be they crewmen or townsfolk or any others that might chance by, not even mentionin' the possibilities of sorcery and black magic as might be involved. You were with the captain at Little Hengist, weren't you?"

He blinked at me, and looked about as if he expected to see the Sorcerer's creatures climbing up the rigging, and then he turned back to me and said, "Very well, Mr. Jones, lead the way, then."

I led him straight to the cabin, where the poor captain's body lay and Black Eddie stood guard, and we closed up the sliding trap on the skylight above the map table, and we checked the stern windows and made sure they were tight, and Black Eddie went from one cabinet to the next and made sure that there was nobody tucked away in any of them, neither a crewman tucked small nor the Sorcerer's homunculi, not as we really thought the Sorcerer still gave a tinker's dam for any of us aboard the *Bonny Anne*, but you never know.

And when we were sure that the place was as private as we could make it, I turned to Hasty Bernie and said, "He's dead."

The night air on the ride down to the ship, and the business of getting the corpse aboard and getting ourselves alone and private with Bernie had given my head time to clear, and there wasn't any doubt any more. I'd heard that snap I'd heard, and I knew it for what it was.

Bernie snapped his head around like to break his own neck and stared at that lump on the bunk. "Dead?" he said, "Captain Dancy?"

"Dead as a stone," Black Eddie said. "Whilst Billy was fetchin' you down, I took a look at 'im, and listened for his heart and felt for his pulse, and the man's dead if ever a man was."

"Good Lord," Bernie said, staring at the corpse. "Now what are we going to do?"

I blinked, and looked at Black Eddie, who looked back at me.

"We were hopin'," Eddie pointed out to Bernie, "that *you* could tell *us* that."

"Me?" Bernie looked from one of us to the other and back, with a look on him as if we'd just suggested he bugger the Governor's pet penguin.

"You *are* in command," Eddie said mildly.

Bernie looked at us each, desperately, and then crossed to the bunk and knelt. "You're *sure* he's dead?" he asked.

We both nodded, but Bernie bent down and checked for himself, feeling for a breath from the nose and mouth, listening for the heart, feeling for a pulse, and finding nothing at all.

It was just then that someone knocked at the cabin door, and we looked at one another like as we were schoolboys caught with the maid and her bloomers down, and Black Eddie stared at Hasty Bernie, and Hasty Bernie stared around the room, and after a moment I called, "Who is it?"

"Got a letter for the captain," someone answered.

"Slip it under the door," I said.

The fellow hesitated, and then said, "I don't think I can do that, sir; I was told to give it to Captain Dancy and no other, or it'd be my neck in a noose."

I glanced at the others, but they just shrugged, so I went to the door and opened it.

There stood Jamie McPhee, with the letter in his hand, and I saw the red seal upon it and knew it wasn't just a bill from the chandler nor any such trifle.

"The Captain's ill," I said. "Got a clout on the head in a fight, and that atop a bottle of bad rum, and he's in no shape for readin' a letter. If you'd care to come in and put it in his hand, you'll have done as you were told, but you needn't wait for him to wake; he's dead to the world, and it might be noon before he rises again."

Or it might be Judgment Day, I added to myself.

The boy looked past me at the body on the bunk, and the situation seemed mighty plain, so he shrugged and said, "Well, I done my best, Mr. Jones, and with both you here and Mr. Abernathy there watching I reckon it's right enough. Here's the letter then, and I'm shut of it." And he handed me the letter.

Parchment, it was.

Jamie hurried off, and I closed the door tight and took the letter to Hasty Bernie.

I held it out to him, but he looked at it as if it were a hungry piranha, and at me as if I were straight out of Bedlam. "That's for the Captain," he said.

"And that's you, sir," I said. "Seein' as Captain Dancy's dead."

He stared at it for a moment longer, and I stood there, waiting.

"Oh, all right, damn you," he said, and he snatched the letter away and looked at it.

His face went white.

"Oh, Lord," he said, "It's from Governor Lee."

"Open it," Black Eddie said. "Let's hear the worst."

2.

HIS HANDS shaking, Bernie broke the big red seal and opened it, and he read it aloud, and what it said was this:

> *"Dear Captain Dancy, As you will recall as well as do I, when I granted you Pardon for your Crimes*

this three years past, there were certain Terms agreed upon by us both. Though we have not always seen eye to eye on every Detail, I have, I feel, fully lived up to my end of the Arrangement, and I confess you have done well enough on your own. However, one Provision of our Agreement remains in Doubt. You must surely know to what I refer. Having seen Mistress Coyne twice this fortnight past, how could you not? I trust you will remedy this Oversight forthwith. Should you fail to satisfy me of your good will by this coming Dawn, either by completing our Arrangement or by suitably demonstrating your Intent, I fear I will be required to consider the entire Agreement void, your Pardon revoked, and your ship forfeit to the Crown. Signed, Geo. Lee, Governor.''

When he'd read that, Bernie stared at the paper for a long moment. Then he looked up at Eddie and at me, and said, "Good Christ, whatever is *this* about?"

Eddie and me, we shook our heads, as we hadn't either of us any more idea than a duck.

"Who's this Mistress Coyne, then?" Eddie asked.

"I have no idea," Bernie said.

"Nor do I," said I.

"An' what do we do *now*?" Eddie asked.

"Your ship forfeit to the crown, it says," I remarked. "Seems to me that we'd want to avoid that. I'm not overly concerned about losing the Captain's pardon, as that was for a sentence of death, and he's clear of that, but I'm not eager to lose the ship."

"Could he take it?" Bernie asked thoughtfully. "We've men and guns, after all. We could fight."

"Aye, that we could," I said, "But we'd lose. The Governor's got men and guns himself, aboard the frigate just across the harbor."

"The *Armistead Castle*," Bernie said. "I'd forgot her."

"Aye," I said, "That's the one."

"And the *Castle*'s ready for sea," Eddie pointed out. "I saw meself, they've a full crew aboard, standing a proper watch tonight, not a port watch."

"The Governor must ha' meant that to fright the Captain," I said. "He's lettin' us know he's serious in his threats."

"I don't know about the Captain, but it frightens me right well," Hasty Bernie said. "That frigate's sixteen guns a side; we couldn't possibly stand up to her."

"Aye," Eddie said. "Well then, shall we fetch the men and raise anchor to run? We can be over the horizon by dawn, if we're brisk about it."

"Nay," said I, "For then we'd be fugitives, and shut of Collyport forever, not to mention having all the rest of the Royal Navy after us."

"Well, and aren't we fugitives now?" Eddie asked.

"Not here," said I, "Not with the governor's pardon."

"But that runs out at dawn," Eddie said.

"Not if we show our good intent," I told him.

Bernie was still staring at the parchment, but he said, "Maybe if we just went to the governor and told him what happened. . . ."

"Would he believe us?" I asked.

"We've got the bloody corpse to prove it, ye blidget!" Eddie said. "How could he not?"

"Are ye plannin' to drag the captain all the way up to the governor's palace, then, and haul it in with us when he agrees to see us—*if* he agrees to see us?"

Black Eddie had to think about that one for a moment.

"We might could try it," he said at last, but we knew by the tone that his heart weren't in it. I was ready to mention the Caliburn Witch, and her promise to live and let live only until she heard that Jack Dancy was dead, but I could see Eddie wasn't going to argue, so I held off.

"Why'd the governor want to be so bloody cryptic in his letter, anyway?" Bernie snapped.

"And why'd the captain not tell us what in hell he

149

wanted with that wagon, and what he'd promised the governor?" Black Eddie retorted.

"And when," said I, "Did the captain *ever* tell us what he was up to?"

That silenced them both, for the truth was that Jack Dancy had always been close with his counsel. As he told me once, "Billy," he said, "if you don't tell people what you're planning, they won't worry about what might go wrong." And sure enough, he'd always pulled off everything he'd put his hand to, no matter how bad it looked, no matter how bad it *was*, he'd always pulled it off. Sometimes he only survived by the skin of his teeth, but he always survived, as if all the gods of luck owed him heavily and had interest to pay.

Well, his luck had run out tonight.

And we were standing there looking at one another, the three of us, when the cabin door opened. We heard the hinges creak, and the three of us spun about, and Black Eddie's dirk was out, and my own hand seemed to be on the hilt of me own dagger, and there we all were, staring at Miss Melissa, who was by her face just as surprised to see us as we were to see her.

"Good evenin' to ye, gentlemen," she said. "Is the captain in?"

Eddie and I looked at one another, and then at Hasty Bernie, who swallowed and said, "Miss Melissa, there's bad news."

"Oh? Is he drunk, Mr. Abernathy?" She looked at the body on the bunk and stepped into the cabin.

Bernie looked at the two of us, but we were no help to him, and his face twisted up. "Worse," he said.

Miss Melissa gave him a look such as I hope I never have to endure. "He's hurt, then?" she asked, closing the door behind her.

"Dead," said Black Eddie.

"Dead?" She was at the bunk before I could blink, tipping the corpse's head back for a good look.

For a moment, we all just stood and watched her, as she saw what we'd all seen. Then she let out a great sob.

"Damn you, Jack Dancy!" she said, her back still to us, and her voice weren't steady at all. "What the hell did you go and die for? Eddie, go get Doc Brewer—he was down in the after hold last I saw, counting those masks we got at Pennington's Cay."

Black Eddie threw a look at Hasty Bernie, who nodded, and then Eddie trotted out the door.

Miss Melissa turned, and we could see the tears running down her face, and it seemed I felt my own throat thickening and my eyes going damp. All that strong drink must have numbed me, a bit, for surely the captain's death was enough to make a man cry, but it wasn't until I saw Miss Melissa weeping that it came home to me.

"How did it happen, Billy?" she asked me.

I shrugged, and said, "He fell. Hit his head on a brick wall, and his neck snapped."

She stared at me, and the tears stopped.

"That's *all*?" she asked.

I nodded. "That's all," I said.

"That son of a bitch!" she said. "You mean it wasn't the Governor's men? Nor the Sorcerer? Nor the Pundit? Nor the *Amber Lassie*? Nor 'Tholomew Sanchez?"

"No," I said, "Wasn't any of those. He slipped and fell while drunk, and that's all there was to it."

"Well, I'll . . . a man like Jack Dancy, dead like that?"

I nodded.

"That's not fitting. It's a damn poor ending to a life like that!"

"I'd agree with that," I said, and Bernie nodded.

For a moment the three of us stood silent, thinking about the captain. It was Miss Melissa who broke the quiet.

"What were his last words, then?" she asked me. "Did he leave us with a fine speech to remember him?"

I had to think about that. We'd been in Old Joe's, and we'd just beaten those sailors and were on our way out through the back, and Jack Dancy had turned to me, smiling and drunk.

"His last words," I said, "were, 'Billy, I'm going to need five guineas later tonight; have you got 'em?' "

Miss Melissa glared at me like as I'd belched in church. "That's a hell of a way to go out, asking for money!"

I didn't argue any. Instead, I said, "I think there's something you'd best be seein', Miss Melissa." I pointed to the governor's letter.

Bernie handed it to her, and she read it, and then she looked up and asked, "Who's Mistress Coyne?"

"We don't know," I said. "That's just what we were askin' amongst ourselves when you came in."

She squinted at me suspiciously, and I looked her in the eye because I wasn't doing anything but telling the simple truth. "D'ye think Jack was bedding her?" she asked me.

I shrugged. "I don't know, Miss Melissa," I said. "I truly don't. I never heard her name until this letter arrived, not half an hour ago."

"Miss Melissa," Bernie said, "while I understand your concern with the mysterious Mistress Coyne, might I point out that it's rather more urgent that we discover just what promises Captain Dancy made to Governor Lee, than whether he'd been . . . ah. . . ."

"Than whether he'd been tomcatting about again," she finished for him. "You mean you don't *know* what the promise was?"

"No," Bernie said.

She looked at me, and I shook my head.

"Nor I," I said.

"Well," she said, looking at the letter. "We can't ask the governor, for he'd not have the likes of us in his palace."

I threw Bernie a glance, and shook my head as he started to open his mouth. There was no need for her to know that we'd been in the palace half a dozen times with Jack Dancy, going in by way of the caves 'round the other side of Collins Island that led into the wine cellars. Nor did she need to be told that Captain Dancy had once walked in the front gate at the governor's invitation. The circumstances for that one didn't bear telling to the captain's lady.

"So that means we'll have to see this Mistress Coyne," Miss Melissa announced.

I blinked.

"Beggin' your pardon," I said, "but how are we to do that? We don't know who she is, or where, and we've no more than five hours to dawn, I'd judge, when the governor's said the ship's to be forfeit."

"Well," Miss Melissa said, "It seems plain to me that *somebody* knows who she is and where she's to be found. You tell me that you two don't know, but someone aboard might. Did Jack go alone when he saw her, without word to any? And even if he did, there's the governor who knows who and where she is, and the governor's spies who told him that Jack had been to see her; can't we ask them?"

"Well, we can't ask the governor, can we?" I said.

"And half the crew's out carousing," Bernie pointed out.

"Well, then, what about the governor's spies?" Miss Melissa asked.

I had to think about that. Something seemed familiar there.

"Mr. Abernathy," I said, speaking slowly so as to think about what I was saying, "Wa'n't it one of the governor's men who brought you that bottle on Sunday?"

The bottle I referred to had had an imp in it once, and the captain had wanted it for a deal he was making with the vengeful brother of the harbormaster's first wife, but that's beside the point.

"Aye," Hasty Bernie said, "It was. What of it?"

Miss Melissa looked at me. "D'you think, then, that this man might know where we can find the wench?"

I shrugged. "He might, and what better have we got to do, than to ask him?"

"D'you know where he's to be found, then?" she asked.

"No," I said, "But I know who does."

It was at that moment that Black Eddie flung open the door and stepped in, with Doc Brewer close on his heels—and Peter Long the bo'sun right behind Doc Brewer.

"Here, you can't come in!" Bernie called at Peter. "The captain's ill!"

"Oh," Peter said, taking in the lump on the bunk and noticing who he was following. He stopped with his toes on the sill. "Well, then, tell the captain I've got his parrot."

Hasty Bernie blinked in surprise, and Miss Melissa stared, and I asked, "*What* parrot?"

"The one he sent me after, Billy. He told me to go up to the Hightown Market and buy the big parrot from the one-eyed bugger in the red and gold tent, and I did, and I've got the damn bird in the fo'c'sle, and it like to bit me nose off."

"All right, Peter," said I. "If he didn't hear that himself I'll be sure to tell him, you've my word on it."

"Thank ye, Billy. I've no fancy to keep the bird myself." He tipped his cap, and turned away.

Black Eddie and Doc Brewer had been standing in the cabin listening to this, and when Peter was gone and Doc was closing the cabin door, Black Eddie said, "A *parrot*?"

"I've no more of it than you, Eddie," I said.

"Doctor," Miss Melissa said, paying no attention to Eddie and myself. "The captain's dead, and there's no doubt of it, so it's not your medical skills that we wanted. It's necromancy, and you're the man aboard that knows most of magicks, so I sent for you."

"Dead?" Doc Brewer started, and turned to the bunk.

"Yes, he's dead, damn him!" Miss Melissa snapped, with her hands on her hips and fire in her eye. A pretty thing, she was then.

"Miss Melissa. . . ." Bernie started to say, but at a glare from her, he thought better of it.

Doc Brewer wasn't listening. He was inspecting Jack Dancy's remains, poking at the neck with his fingers and muttering to himself.

"Whacked his head, he did," he said. "Snapped the third cervical vertebra, and the severed edge went right through the spinal cord, by the look of it. He probably never felt a thing."

That was some comfort to me, hearing that.

Doc muttered on for a moment, whilst the rest of us gradually lost interest in talking and got to watching and listening. Finally, Doc straightened up and said, "He may not even know he's dead, it was so quick. If that's the fact, then the chances are good that his ghost is still back where he died, trying to ascertain what's happened to him. A witch might be able to locate the spirit and converse with it, but earthbound souls aren't anything I can handle."

Miss Melissa started to protest, but Doc Brewer held up a hand to silence her. "On the other hand," he said, "Jack Dancy was a sharp man, and a realist, and he may have seen what happened and know he's dead. In that case, there's no telling what's become of him, whether he's earthbound or on to his final rest or somewhere in between. If he's yet in limbo, I can bespeak him, and if he's in hell, which I pray he's not, for rogue that he was I liked the man and I thought well of him . . . well, if he's in hell, I may be able to reach him but it's not sure. If he's gone to the reward of the blessed, alas, though *he'll* be happy, *we* won't, for if that's the case he's beyond all earthly concerns and can't be reached by any means known to mortal man save direct divine intercession—and I've no knack for that, let me tell you! The Pope himself can't rely on it!"

Hasty Bernie snorted. "Of course he can't," he said. "He's an old fraud, no holier than I am, and his whole church. . . ." He caught sight of our faces and stopped.

Black Eddie's a Papist, of course, and we all knew it, and Hasty Bernie had no call to speak ill of the Bishop of Rome in front of Eddie that way, but his own faith had got the better of him for a moment.

We didn't hold it against him, though, and Miss Melissa carried on, asking Doc, "So you might be able to reach him and ask him what his agreement with the governor was?"

Doc was puzzled by that. "The governor?"

Miss Melissa handed him the letter, and he read it.

"I don't know," he said, handing it back, "but I'll see what I can do. I'd best prepare my spells—the sooner the better."

We could none of us argue with that, so we stood politely as the doc left.

When the door closed behind him, Miss Melissa turned to me and said, "You were sayin' that you can find the governor's man, who might lead us to this Mistress Coyne?"

"Not I," I replied. "But Jamie McPhee, as he handles errands like that for the captain."

"Let's get on with it, then," she said. "Have him in here and get *on* with it!"

"Couldn't we wait until the doctor. . . ." Bernie began, but Miss Melissa cut him off with a glare.

"Now, Mr. Abernathy," I said. "You heard what Doc Brewer told us; it's as like as not he can't contact the captain. And we've no time to waste in trying. Eddie, can ye call the lad?"

Black Eddie nodded and stepped out, and the rest of us stood about fiddling our thumbs, staring each at the other and thinking on what we should do.

3.

WE HAD none of us come up with anything when Jamie arrived, of himself, without a sign of Black Eddie. We sent him to talk to the governor's man and find out who this Mistress Coyne might be.

"Why?" he asked.

Hasty Bernie started to say, "Well, lad, the Captain. . . ."

Miss Melissa hushed him. "It's not your concern, boy," she said. "And we've no time to explain. You just go and ask, and come back here quick!"

He nodded, and hurried out.

We all looked after him as he left. Hasty Bernie remarked, "Collyport's a rough place by night; I hope he'll have no problems."

"Ah, the lad knows the town," I said. "There's nothing to worry about."

"Nothing to worry about!" Hasty Bernie shouted, glaring at me. "The Governor's about to claim the ship, the captain's dead, and not one of us even knows what's happening—and you tell us not to worry?"

"Well," I said. "What good did worry ever do a man? There's naught more to be done until we hear from the lad or Doc Brewer, is there? Then there's nothing *we* can do, and no reason to worry!"

"An odd philosophy," Hasty Bernie said.

"A fool's philosophy," Miss Melissa retorted. "How do we know there's naught can be done? What if the doctor can't reach the captain, nor the boy find this Mistress Coyne? Are we to give up the ship without a fight, and starve in the streets?"

"Oh, we'd not starve," I said. "A man who'd sailed

with Jack Dancy can surely find another berth! But I'd as soon keep the ship, I'll agree with that."

"Is it ours to keep, though?" Hasty Bernie asked, suddenly thoughtful. "Did the captain own it? Who are his heirs?"

"*We* are," Miss Melissa snapped. "Who else could there be?"

"I thought his family," Bernie began. "His children. . . ."

"*What* family?" Miss Melissa shouted. "He swore he'd never married!"

"Nor did he," I told her.

"Then what children?" she demanded triumphantly.

"Miss Melissa," I said, "you must know better than that. By last count he knew of thirty-one, he told me this Sunday past, and he's been the sole support of the seven whose mothers aren't presently married. And there's a sister back in Weymouth. The captain spoke of her often—she's married to a chandler by the name of Wiggins, I understand."

Her mouth fell open and she stared wide-eyed at me.

"I suppose that Mrs. Wiggins would be the heir of record," Bernie said, "given the lack of a marriage. But did Captain Dancy truly own the ship himself, or did he have a backer?"

"Thirty-one?" Miss Melissa squeaked.

"Or thereabouts," I told her. "You'll understand, the captain often took the lass's word, and I'll not swear they were all of them entirely truthful. But then he may have missed a few, as well, so I'd judge as it might balance out."

"*Thirty-one bastards?*" she shrieked at me.

"Or thereabouts," I repeated.

She stared at me, and Hasty Bernie asked, "Do you think Mrs. Wiggins would know if there were a backer? I'll need to send her a letter in any case, so I thought. . . ."

"*Who cares?*" Miss Melissa screamed, turning to Bernie. "Who cares about any sister, or backer, or the thirty-one bleeding bastards that son of a bitch left? *We're* the ones who *have* the ship, and I don't intend to let the Governor or anybody else take it away! Call the men to their stations—we'll take this ship out and sink anyone who tries to stop us!''

I looked at Bernie, but he was looking helplessly back at me. ''Miss Melissa,'' I said, ''I don't want to lose the *Bonny Anne* any more than you do, nor will we if we can help it, but there's no need for all that, now. The doc's trying to bespeak the captain, and Jamie's gone to find us Mistress Coyne, and there's still a fine hope that we'll be able to keep the Governor's pardon *and* the ship, safe here in Collyport. If ye must do *something*, you'd be better to see if you can think what the Captain promised the Governor, not sending the men to stations.''

''Well said, Mr. Jones,'' Hasty Bernie said. ''Though I still think that determining the ship's rightful owner. . . .''

''Can wait,'' I said, interrupting him. ''Whoever owns her surely won't be wantin' her forfeit to the Crown, and if we can hold her free, we'll be in a position to bargain when the time comes. First, though, we've to hold her free.''

''Aye,'' Bernie admitted.

''And to do that, we've to know what the Governor wants.''

''Or to get out of Collyport,'' Miss Melissa said.

''And go where?'' I asked her, as sweetly as I could. ''In a ship forfeit to the Crown, every English-speakin' port will be closed to us as fast as the word can reach them—and every *other* port is *already* closed to the *Bonny Anne*!''

''All right, then,'' she said. ''What does the Governor want?''

''I've no idea,'' I admitted. ''But the Captain did, and he'd made arrangements, it seems.''

''What arrangements?'' she asked.

''Well,'' I told her, ''Black Eddie was to have a freight wagon at the ship by midnight, and it's there on the dock now. Peter Long was to fetch a particular parrot, and he's got it in the fo'c'sle. It might be there are other things as well that I've not happened on yet."

"A freight wagon?"

I nodded. I didn't mention that we'd used it to fetch the captain's corpse in.

"And a parrot?"

I nodded again.

There was a knock at the door.

We looked at one another, and then Miss Melissa called, "Come in!"

The door opened, and there was Black Eddie with a scrawny little ape of a man I'd never clapped eyes on before. Before Eddie could speak, the stranger barked at us, "If ye'd changed yer damned plans, ye might 'a' had the courtesy to ha' told me!"

"See here, man," Hasty Bernie said. "Who are you talking to that way?"

"I'm talkin' to *you*, ye pompous twit," he sputtered. "You and yer damned captain, what told me to wait for 'is bloody signal that was due at midnight and he ain't gimme yet! And there he is, sleepin' off a bottle or two, ain't he? Damned if I shouldn't 'a' known it. Bloody idiot. Bloody hell!"

He turned and would have stamped away, save that Black Eddie was in his way, which gave Miss Melissa time to ask, "What signal?"

The stranger turned back and squinted at her, then snapped, "A red light on the mizzen. Didn't the damned fool tell ye?"

She shook her head, and Bernie and I just stood there.

The little man looked over at the captain's mortal remains and snorted. "Reckon he passed out before he got that far. Well, then, d'ye want me to fire that warehouse, or don't ye?"

Bernie and I looked at each other. Miss Melissa started to ask, "*What* warehouse?" but I tapped her shoulder before she'd got a good start on the second word, and she hushed up nicely.

"We're runnin' a little late tonight," I said. "As ye said yourself, the captain's been no help to us." I looked at Bernie.

"Aye, if you could bear with us yet for awhile, we'd appreciate it," he said.

The little man looked us all over and was about to snort again when I said, "Listen, man, you go back to your post and gi' us ten more minutes beyond. If the red light's not up by then, belay the whole job and go home to your bed with our blessings. There's an extra silver guinea for your trouble. Fair enough?" I fished the coin from me purse and held it up. Didn't leave me much, but he didn't look the sort to settle for a shilling.

He squinted again, then said, "Fair enough. Hand it over."

I obliged him, and he tucked the guinea away, and Black Eddie led him back to the rail.

Miss Melissa watched him over the side, then slammed the door and spun on us.

"What in hell was *that* about?" she asked.

Hasty Bernie shrugged.

"Seems to me," I said, "as the captain had a diversion planned. A big one. And I'll wager I know what warehouse it is, too, as Jack Dancy was always a man to get the most for his efforts."

Bernie blinked. Miss Melissa stared at me for a moment, and then a smile spread across her face.

"Sanchez?" she asked.

I nodded. "He's out to sea now, but he's got a good lot of his booty tucked away where he didn't figure it to be shot up if he meets an unfriendly ship. Wasn't worth our while doin' a thing to it in the ordinary course, but if it's a diversion we need anyway, why, there 'tis ready to go."

"But what do we need a diversion *for*?" Bernie asked, his face troubled.

"I don't know," I said. "But we have ten minutes to decide whether we need one at all."

"If Jack arranged it, we'll probably need it," Miss Melissa said, and I had to agree that that was generally true.

"There's a freight wagon," I said. "And this letter from the Governor, and visits to Mistress Coyne, and now a fire to be set as a diversion just as the freight wagon was to be here."

"And a parrot," Bernie added.

"And a bloody damn parrot," I agreed. "With all that, then, does either of you have any notion of just what might be goin' on?"

They looked at each other, and then back at me.

"No," Bernie said.

"Seems to me," I said slowly, "that a diversion over at the warehouse is meant to draw attention away from the ship. If it were a diversion elsewhere that the captain wanted, he could have made it himself ready enough right here, or any number of ways."

"If it really *is* a diversion," Miss Melissa suggested.

I considered that, while Bernie protested, "Captain Dancy wouldn't burn down that warehouse just for spite! And why on a signal from the ship, if he just wanted it done?"

"Maybe not a *diversion*," I said, "so much as *cover*. Now, the captain must have planned on being here aboard ship at midnight, so as to give the signal, and to do whatever was to be done with the freight wagon. Suppose that you're aboard your ship, and you see a fire over there on the great wharf—what do you do?"

"I put out to sea, of course," Bernie said. "To get clear of sparks."

"D'ye think, then, that Jack was going to run?" Miss Melissa asked. "He was no coward!"

I shook my head. "No, not Jack Dancy. He wouldn't ha' run from Governor Lee, nor from the *Armistead Castle*, nor from the devils of Hell. Nor would he give up Collyport so easy. So if he'd knowed what the Governor was on about in that letter, and that this was the night he had to deliver, he'd ha' done his damnedest to deliver. So he planned on doing it from the sea, somehow."

"What about the wagon?" Bernie asked. "Maybe he figured on sending the ship to sea, so that everyone would think he was gone, and all the while he'd be about his business with the wagon."

"No, Mr. Abernathy," I said. "For then he'd want the *Bonny Anne*'s departure noted, and he'd 'a' had us sail out in broad daylight, not put out at midnight to escape a fire. No, the fire's to give us a reason for leaving harbor at night, I'm sure of it."

I had an idea, then, of where the captain might have had in mind to go, but I didn't know the why of it yet at all.

There'd be no point in leaving at midnight if we were to be bound for another island; we couldn't reach another that night, and if we'd a need to reach another at a particular time it would be easier to make the time right along the way than by sailing out in the dark. Even in a harbor we knew as well as that one, sailing out at night is a bit of a risk.

So we were going somewhere else on Collins Island, somewhere that was best reached by sea, and where he didn't want us to be seen, and where we *would* have been seen if we'd sailed there by day, and somewhere that wasn't close enough to row there easy in the ship's launch.

I knew what that meant, plain enough. The Captain had meant to sail around to the caves.

But why?

If he'd meant to meet with someone there, then we were bound to miss it entirely, as it was more than an hour after midnight and we hadn't even got most of the crew aboard, as far as I knew.

But then, if someone was waiting in the caves for us, he weren't about to go much of anywhere in any hurry, as the cliffs above and to the sides were a mighty rough climb, and the cliff below led nowhere but the sea.

There was the other end of the cave, of course, but there weren't many as knew about that.

All the same, if we were to have met someone there, he might be there yet by the time we could reach him, or he might not, and I'd have been much happier if I'd have known just what to expect.

I wished as Jamie McPhee would hurry back.

Someone knocked at the door, and I thought as my wish had been granted, but then Black Eddie called from without, "It's been nigh on ten minutes."

"Aye," I said, and then I called, "Send up the signal! And prepare for sea!" Boldness, Captain Dancy used to tell me, boldness will win sooner than wit.

"What?" Miss Melissa shrieked at me, and I looked at her quite reproachful, as it hurt my ear.

"Mr. Jones," Bernie said. "Billy, do you know just what you're doing?"

"Not entirely," I confessed. "But I have a fair to middlin' idea."

"What about Jamie?" Miss Melissa asked, still shouting, but not half as loud.

"I'll send a man to fetch him," Bernie said.

"I'd not waste the time," I said. "Beggin' your pardon, Mr. Abernathy. But what you might do is put a boat over, and leave it by the dock with a couple of men aboard, to row the lad out to us when he arrives."

Bernie stared at me thoughtful for a moment, then nodded, and he left the cabin to see to it.

That left me, and Miss Melissa, and the corpse, and when I realized I was the only living man there with her, my tongue dried out and of a sudden I found nothing to say.

She hadn't the same problem, though.

"And who do you think you are, Billy Jones, to be ordering about Mr. Abernathy and doing what you please?"

"I'm second mate of this ship, Miss Melissa," I answered her. "And I'm just doin' what I can to see us all safe, now that the captain's not here to do it."

She looked me in the eye for a moment, and I didn't blink. Then she turned away and looked at the captain's body and whispered, "Damn you, Jack Dancy!"

Then she turned again and marched out.

4.

I COVERED up the captain and tried to make him look natural, just in case someone should chance to look in, and as I was about to go up on deck there was old Wheeler coming in, about to whine about somewhat or the other, and thinking quick I held up a finger to hush him.

"The Captain's bad tonight," I told him. "Don't you touch him, unless you want to kiss the gratings tomorrow!"

Wheeler nodded, and went about his business, throwing a glance over his shoulder every so oft, but not going near the corpse.

I just hoped the captain wouldn't start to stink too soon. Maybe Doc Brewer could do something about that.

Then I went up, and at first I thought that dawn was breaking and we'd wasted the whole night, but then I saw as this light was orange, and not the pink of dawn at all, and I realized as it was the warehouse on fire.

Around us, other ships were casting off, their crews running about and shouting. I could see the *Armistead Castle* spreading canvas already. She had a good crew, that ship.

And there aboard the *Bonny Anne* about me were the men and boys hanging in the rigging and watching the fire, and chattering amongst themselves like so many gulls, and the ship still at the dock!

I looked about and saw Hasty Bernie on the quarter-deck, staring up the streets of Collyport, and I was as angry with him as I'd ever been. "Hey!" I called. "You bloody damn fools, that's a fire over there, and there'll be sparks in the air, and our sails could catch! Cast off! Get us out to sea!"

I saw Peter Long throw a look at Hasty Bernie, but Bernie just nodded, and a moment later we were making way, pulling away from Collyport on the westerly airs.

I saw that at least Bernie had put down a boat, with Black Eddie in it, lest Jamie should happen along. And I saw that those other ships were putting out, as well. The *Bonny Anne* would be second or third out of the harbor, behind the *Armistead Castle* and maybe a merchantman off to starboard.

And the sparks *were* blowing in the wind and coming after us, and I didn't like it at all, and as I called the orders to work the sails I made sure to send a boy below for buckets and lines. It was just like the captain, to have come up with a diversion that could burn the ship!

It was only when we were safe out at sea that I took the time to think about anything but getting the *Bonny Anne* clear, and looked about.

There was Bernie on the quarterdeck—as I was myself, I noticed, having come up and taken the wheel without thinking about it. Miss Melissa was beside Hasty Bernie, and the two of them were arguing in whispers. I didn't trouble myself about just why, as yet. The rest of the crew, those as were aboard, were going about their business as they should, despite it being the middle of the night and near as black as the Sorcerer's soul.

Now it seemed to me as the time had come to decide what to do. The captain's plan called for sailing around the island to the caves, I was sure, but did we really want to do that?

Well, I supposed we did, as why else were we at sea?

I looked over at Mr. Abernathy and the captain's lady and decided that I'd best not bother them about it, as it would only mean more argument. I turned the wheel and put her on the starboard tack.

She was turning sweetly when I heard a hail from the masthead.

Our boat was coming out from the harbor, with Jamie McPhee and Black Eddie and, the lookout swore, a woman in the bow.

"Heave to," I called, "and bring 'em aboard!"

The men went to it with a will, and that boat seemed to skim right up to us in a mighty pretty piece of rowing, so it wasn't but a few minutes before we had the boat up out of the water and Jamie and Eddie and the woman on the halfdeck.

And sure enough they had a woman with them, a tall, comely thing, with red hair free to her waist and wearing a red and gold gown to go with it. She had a wide-brimmed red velvet hat on her head, with a veil all around, and white gloves to her hands, which seemed a little more than was purely necessary for the weather.

I called the orders to get us under way again whilst Jamie and Eddie brought her up to the quarterdeck. They took her over to Hasty Bernie, as he was the senior officer aboard, but I caught Eddie's eye and gestured for him to take the wheel.

"We're bound for the caves," I whispered to him. "Fast as we can get there without riskin' the rocks."

He nodded and grabbed the spokes, and I slipped over toward the others.

"Mr. Abernathy," Jamie was saying, "this is Mistress Annabelle Coyne."

Hasty Bernie took her hand and bowed, smiled his best formal smile, and then stood there staring at her and looking stupid. 'Twas plain to me that the poor man had no idea what to do. I thought back on the watchbill and realized that he'd most likely been without sleep for nigh onto thirty hours, while I hadn't missed but an hour or two's sleep as yet, so I stepped forward.

I smiled and tipped my hat, once I remembered I was wearing it, as it happens I was, and said, "I'm Billy Jones, Mistress Coyne. Welcome aboard the *Bonny Anne*."

I could see Miss Melissa out of the corner of my eye, and she looked somewhat put out, both with Bernie and myself, but I didn't worry about that as yet.

"Thank you, Mr. Jones," said Mistress Coyne.

"My apologies, Mistress Coyne," Bernie said. "It seems I need Mr. Jones to remind me of my manners. Welcome, indeed, and thank you for coming."

Miss Melissa glared at Bernie, and I knew that Mistress Coyne saw it; wasn't no love lost between those two women, be sure of that!

"Thank *you*, Mr. Abernathy," she said. "But I must confess, I'm not sure why I am here."

Bernie blinked at that, and he and I both looked at Jamie.

"She wouldn't say a thing to me," Jamie blurted out. "So's I brought her."

"Ah," Bernie said.

Miss Melissa suggested, "Jamie, tell us what happened."

He glanced about, but there wasn't any there as didn't want him to speak, so he spoke. "Well, you sent me to talk to a man I know and ask as to who Mistress Coyne was, and I did that, and he told me as he didn't know a thing about her, save where she lived and what she looked like, and that she was at the governor's palace every so often, and that the governor was at her place on occasion, and as the two of them sent notes back and forth. And I figured as that probably wasn't all you'd wanted me to find out, so I asked for more, and he swore as how that was all he knew, but he could show me her place, and I said as I'd be pleased if he did, so he did, and there she was, and I was looking in the door—it's a little tea-room that she runs. Anyway, I was looking in the door, and she saw me and asked me what I wanted, and I didn't know as what I should say, and she asked who I was, and I told her, and she asked as who sent me, and I said that I was from the *Bonny Anne*, and she asked as whether Captain Dancy had wanted something of her, and I allowed as how I hadn't any idea, and then she asked if the ship was in port, and I said of course it was or I wouldn't be there, and next thing I knew she was coming with me back to the ship to see what was happening, and here we are.''

He stopped as if the words had run out sooner than he'd expected, and had surprised him in doing it, and he sort of blinked at us in confusion.

''Thank you, lad,'' Bernie said. He turned to Mistress Coyne and asked, ''It seems to me, mistress, that you came here of your own will, and that you know why better than we.''

''I'll tell you what I know, Mr. Abernathy,'' she replied tartly. ''I know that Captain Dancy had told me his ship would be leaving port at midnight, and here it is after that when a boy turns up at my shop saying that the *Bonny Anne* is still in port, and with a tale of being sent to find out who I am, when Jack Dancy has known me well these several months past. So I came to see what's become of the captain. I'd hoped to see him here on his own quarterdeck, and instead I find you in command. Could you tell me why?''

Bernie harrumphed—did a fine job of it, too, rocking back on his heels. ''Well, mistress,'' he said. ''As it happens, the captain is indisposed. Very much so, I'm afraid. Our ship's doctor, Emmanuel Brewer, is tending to him now.''

Mistress Coyne said, in a very quiet voice, ''I'm sorry to hear that.''

''So were we,'' Bernie replied. ''And after he was taken ill, we had word from Governor Lee that he was concerned over some agreement he had made with the captain. The message was not at all clear, I fear, but it did let us know that the Governor took the matter, whatever it is, very seriously. Being loyal subjects of the Crown, we wanted to do our best to carry on despite the captain's temporary inconvenience—but I'm afraid the captain had neglected to inform any of us of just what it was the Governor wanted. However, your name was mentioned in the Governor's message, so we thought perhaps you could shed a little light on the situation.''

''I see,'' said Mistress Coyne. I looked away for a moment to judge our position—the cliffs to port loomed up black and appeared a good bit closer than I really cared to see them.

When I looked back Mistress Coyne was lifting her veil, and the light from the mizzen lantern caught her face full. I swallowed and tried not to stare.

It was plain to me in that instant why she had worn a veil; a face like that isn't to be risked parading openly through the streets of Collyport at night.

''Jack Dancy didn't tell you *anything*?'' she asked.

We all shook our heads—Bernie, Miss Melissa, myself, even Jamie.

''Jamie, run along and get some sleep,'' I said, now that I'd recalled he was there.

The others turned to stare as Jamie started a protest, and when he met all those eyes he thought better of arguing. He shuffled away, disappointed.

''You've not mutinied, have you?'' Mistress Coyne asked, once Jamie was clear.

Bernie and I were honestly shocked, but I saw as how she could think it might be. We both spoke at once, but I think we made it plain we'd done no such a thing.

Mistress Coyne looked about, and asked, ''Where are we? Where are you taking me?''

Bernie started to say something about how it wasn't her concern, but I spoke up and said, ''We're bound to a place we know of around the other side of the island. The captain told us that much, though we were late on gettin' a start.''

''Do you know what you're to do there?''

170

"No."

She nodded. "I see." She studied us, and then looked Miss Melissa straight in the eye and asked, "And who might you be?"

Miss Melissa took a deep, angry breath and turned red as a boiled lobster. Bernie spoke up before she could shout, though.

"This is Mistress Melissa Dewhurst, a good friend of Captain Dancy and aboard the *Bonny Anne* at the captain's personal invitation."

"I'm delighted to meet you, Mistress Dewhurst," Mistress Coyne said with a nod, "But I fear that you must be bored by all this chatter?"

Miss Melissa drew another breath, but this time 'twas myself who stopped her.

"Miss Melissa," I said, "I'd take it as a great favor if you would go below and see whether there's been any change in the captain's condition." And I pointed to the cabin skylight.

She nodded, and gave Mistress Coyne a look such as I hope I never receive from any woman, and then marched off the quarterdeck.

Once she was gone I kept an eye on the cabin skylight, lest Miss Melissa be clumsy in opening it to hear, while Bernie asked, "Now, Mistress Coyne, if you don't mind, is there anything you can tell us?"

She looked about dubiously, and saw that the only people on the quarterdeck were herself, and Bernie, and me, and Black Eddie at the wheel. She could hardly expect the helmsman to leave his post, and Bernie and I were the captain's two senior officers and two of his closest friends. None of the men in the rigging were close to hand.

"I don't know the details of Captain Dancy's plan," she said. "But I do know what Governor Lee wants of him. He's to remove Madame Lee."

Bernie looked puzzled. "Remove Madame Lee?" he repeated.

Mistress Coyne nodded.

"Remove how?"

"Alive."

That was some relief, in any case; I'd no particular desire to kill a woman, and besides, it hardly made sense to hire a man like Jack Dancy as a mere assassin. There's many a simpler way for a man to kill his own wife, should he care to.

There'd been that fellow on Pennington's Cay, for one— but no, that wasn't all that much simpler at that, and not relevant to the present case.

I tried to recall what I'd heard of Madame Lee.

The Governor had brought her back from another island five years before, and had held a wedding that was still the subject of many a barroom tale or boast, though there wasn't but two people actually killed that day, and at least one of them clearly deserved it. I'd no idea what her maiden name might have been, or which island she'd come from, nor for that matter of much else about her. I'd never laid eyes on her, nor had any man I knew of, not to swear to. I knew precious little about her, if the truth be known.

There were rumors, of course, but I'd not put faith in rumors, after some as I'd heard where I knew the truth of the matter. Why, the rumors would have it that Jack Dancy . . . well, they lied, and enough of that.

But as to the discussion we were having with Mistress Coyne, the next word spoken came from Mr. Abernathy.

"Why?" Bernie asked, and in my heart I cursed the man for a fool. Hadn't he heard what Jamie had said? Hadn't he seen Mistress Coyne's face? It was as plain to me as I might want that the Governor had it in mind to keep company with Mistress Coyne, and for that sort of entertainment the presence of a previous wife can hamper one a mite.

"Why alive, do you mean?" Mistress Coyne asked, and I realized perhaps Bernie wasn't the fool I thought, as it was a sound question. As I said, there's many a simpler way for a man to kill his own wife, and in particular when the man is the governor and chief magistrate of a crown colony, and none's to argue if he says his wife fell from a cliff and wasn't pushed, or that the meal she died of was rotten but not poisoned.

But then I saw Bernie's face, and knew that he *was* a fool. He started to say, "No, I meant—" but I cut him off.

"Aye," I said. "It seems to me as that's a sound question."

"Well, because . . . well, there are reasons that. . . ." She stopped, cross with herself, and started over. "I don't know for certain why the Governor wants her taken alive, but I do know something about her that might have something to do with it."

I nodded, "And what might that be?"

Mistress Coyne grimaced. She said, "Madame Lee is a witch."

5.

HASTY BERNIE and I looked at each other, and we each saw the dismay in the other's eyes.

We had both battled the Black Sorcerer with Jack Dancy. We were both beside him when he fought the devil-kites at Bethmoora, and when the night thing came aboard in Dunvegan Sound. Bernie was there when he outwitted the Pundit of Oul. I was there when he sweet-talked the ship and the lives of a dozen men, myself among them, away from the Caliburn Witch. We'd both seen Doc Brewer work a few little spells, and even those could be enough to terrify any sane man. And we'd both seen enough of other magic to know that neither of us cared to see more.

The prospect of kidnapping a witch was not exactly one that cheered the either of us.

And here we were with little choice, when it came right down to bottom, but to do that very thing. In fact, we were already asail toward the caves, and I knew now why. It wasn't to meet anyone, there was no rendezvous we'd missed; it was because through the caves we could get into the Governor's Palace and catch Madame Lee and bring her out the same way without being seen and without stumbling across the palace guards, as we might have done by any other route.

That is, unless the captain had been planning something complicated, as he might have been, but as we had no way of knowing.

I thought about it for a moment.

The warehouse fire was to get us out to sea without arousing suspicion—and so as to provide an alibi, as well, for later on, should anyone be looking into the matter of Madame Lee's disappearance, Jack Dancy could swear that he and his ship weren't even in the harbor at the time, so how could he be involved?

And Mistress Coyne and the Governor's letter fit in, as well. I judged that Mistress Coyne and Governor Lee had got a mite impatient with the impediments they'd been encountering and wanted the captain to get on with it.

After all, if Governor Lee had made his arrangements with the captain *three years ago*. . . .

The patience of the man would fair qualify him for sainthood, if that were the truth of it, but thinking it over I saw as it wasn't likely that the whole plan had been made that long ago. Not many's the man that keeps the same mistress *and* the same wife so long as that. Besides, the governor had only been married two years at that point, which seems a tad hasty in tiring of a wife. No, my guess was that the governor's agreement with the captain was merely that at some time the governor would set the captain a task to discharge his debt, and that this was the task he'd come up with.

And a task worthy of Jack Dancy's talents it was, too, kidnapping a witch. Even *he* hadn't attempted it before.

I wished Jack Dancy were still alive to do it.

So the fire was accounted for, and the letter—but how did the freight wagon fit in? And the parrot?

Had we taken the wagon on board or left it on the dock? I couldn't for the life of me recall just at that moment, though I didn't recollect any order to bring it aboard, nor seeing it anywhere but the dock. I hoped it didn't matter, but I feared it did. Seeing as the captain had said the wagon was to be there at midnight, and as the fire was to be set near about midnight, I judged as we should already have done something with that damned wagon, either taken it aboard or done something with it back at the dock.

"Beggin' your pardon, Mistress Coyne," I asked, "but would you have any notion as to what use a freight wagon might be in this little enterprise we're attemptin'?"

She considered that for a moment, and then said, "No."

"I feared as much," I told her. "What about a parrot?"

She looked at me as if I were daft and asked, "What *about* a parrot?"

"Ah," I said, "Never you mind." It was plain that the captain hadn't told her any more than he had us, as to the exact details.

There wasn't much more to be done on deck until we reached the caves, so Bernie and I made some polite chit-chat with Mistress Coyne for a moment, and then I slipped away to see just what might be happening elsewhere aboard the *Bonny Anne*.

First off, I saw as the freight wagon wasn't aboard. We'd left it sitting plain on the dock.

I looked into the fo'c'sle, to see the parrot for myself. There it was, on Peter Long's hammock, giving me the beady eye. I called to it, but it wouldn't say a word.

Next I betook myself down to the surgery, where Doc Brewer was sitting cross-legged, naked to the waist and painted like a savage, with black candles burning and a great clutter of skulls and suchlike about him.

He looked up when I came in, and his face was red and puffy, and the sweat was rolling down his chest like rainwater running down the masts. "Hello, Billy," he said.

"I'm not interruptin', am I?" I asked.

He shook his head. "No," he said. "It's of no use. I can't find a trace of him." He got to his feet and leaned against a bulkhead. "It's wearying, it is, calling like that."

I nodded, and tried to think of something sympathetic to say, but before the words came, he asked me, "Where are we bound, Billy? I feel the ship moving. Did you find out what the captain was up to?"

"In a manner of speaking," I admitted. I took a moment to gather my nerve, and then I asked him, "Tell me, could you be handlin' a witch, if we took one prisoner?"

He blinked. "A witch, you say? Are we to capture a witch?"

I nodded. "That we are."

He turned and poked at a canvas bag that hung on the bulkhead. "That would explain this, I suppose."

"Would it, now?" I asked. "And what might that be?"

"Oh, the hide of a salamander, and the bones of an eel, and a variety of other things. The captain told me the day before yesterday to find what I'd need for making a geas, the strongest I knew how. I suppose he meant for me to put a geas on her not to harm us, or some such a requirement."

"And you have it all?" I asked. A thought struck me. "You wouldn't need a parrot, would you?"

"A parrot?" He stared at me. "I've no use for a parrot, not for this spell nor any other I know."

"Oh, well," I said, "I was just askin'. So, do you have what you need for this geas, then?"

"Oh, of course," he said. "Save for the hair of the victim."

"Well," I said, "I don't suppose 'twill be any great feat to cut a lock of her hair for you. How long will it take, once you've the hair?"

He pursed his lips and considered that, and I commenced to worry, as I had hoped he'd be telling me 'twould be no time at all. Instead he said, "Well, it would depend on just when I began, but four to six hours, most likely."

"Ah," said I, thinking about what it would be like trying to hold an angry witch prisoner for six hours, with no magic against her. I wondered what the captain had planned. Had he gotten a hank of Madame Lee's hair, somehow, that Doc Brewer should have already had?

I thought he might, at that. I told Doc to get ready to start his spell and then I went back up on deck.

Peter Long met me there and asked, "Mr. Jones, what's to be done with that blasted parrot?"

"Hold onto it," I told him. "We'll no doubt know soon enough." Then I went on to the quarterdeck. Hasty Bernie and Annabelle Coyne were still talking.

"Mistress Coyne," I asked. "Did the captain, by any chance, mention anything to you about Madame Lee's hair?"

She stared at me. "Now how did you know about that, Mr. Jones?" she asked lightly.

"About what, Mistress?" Bernie asked.

"About the hair. I fetched him a handful of hair, taken from Madame Lee's brush—I don't know why. I guessed he was planning to have a wig made for some part of his deceptions."

"And what became of that hair?" I asked.

"Oh, I haven't the faintest notion," she replied. "I gave it to Captain Dancy yesterday."

I closed my teeth hard to hold back a curse. "Mr. Abernathy," I said, "I'm going below, to take a look at the captain's condition."

"Very good, Mr. Jones," Bernie said.

The moment I stepped through the cabin door, Miss Melissa demanded, "What's this about that woman's hair?" She stepped down from the stool under the skylight and glared at me.

"Doc Brewer needs it for a spell," I told her. "To put Madame Lee under a geas."

"Oh," she said.

"It's most likely somewhere in this cabin," I said.

"Do you think old Wheeler would know?" she asked.

That hadn't occurred to me to wonder, and I allowed as how it hadn't. She went and rousted the old man from his hammock, whilst I began opening cabinets and drawers.

Jack Dancy's old servant wasn't at his best just then, roused in the middle of the night, but at last we managed to explain that we were looking for a hank of a lady's hair that the captain had probably hidden somewhere. I hadn't found anything of the sort in my search—though some of the items I *had* found stirred my curiosity a tad. Whatever did the captain need with a playbill for an opera in Southampton? Or a shell carved to the shape of a herring? And where did he get some of those pictures?

Of course, I recognized a few of his souvenirs, like the tip off the narwhal's tooth, and the green pendant he'd got from Madame Kent after Cushgar Corners.

Well, wasn't none of that important just then.

"A lady's hair?" Wheeler asked, and we both nodded, and Miss Melissa shouted at him a little.

He paid her no mind; instead he crossed to a cabinet I hadn't tried yet, and reached around the side, and opened the cabinet door, and then reached in to the hinge and opened that same door again—the door was made in two layers that folded out.

And between those two layers were pinned a hundred locks of hair, each one tied in a ribbon.

And weren't none of them labeled or tagged.

6.

I STARED at those damned locks of hair for a moment, and then I said words that I'd never have said in the presence of Miss Melissa had I remembered she was there. She said some of the same sort herself, though.

A thought struck me, then. Those hundred hanks were all the colors in which one might expect a lady's hair to be found, from ash to black with a bit of a side trip out to red along the way. I've known men as would only take a blonde lassie, or a redhead, but never let it be said that Jack Dancy put any such arbitrary limits upon his interests.

"And what color, then," I asked, "would Madame Lee's hair be?"

There wasn't a soul there who could answer, so I betook myself back to the quarterdeck and put the same question to Mistress Coyne.

"Brown," she told me. "A middling brown."

And wouldn't you know that full forty of those love-locks were of a middling brown? Naturally, Madame Lee wasn't one of the four redheads, nor the lone ash blonde.

And then we were anchored below the caves, and I saw the night was growing old, and there wasn't more time to worry about it. If we were to spirit Madame Lee from the palace before her maids were up and about, we'd to do it right soon.

I gathered up a few things I thought might be of use, and then I stood on the quarterdeck with Bernie whilst the call went round for volunteers for a shore party, and the men began to gather on the halfdeck, and Hastings Abernathy and I eyed each other a bit, each hoping the other would speak first.

Hasty Bernie was the senior, though, so it was his place,

and at last he sighed and said, "One of us must go ashore, Mr. Jones, and the other keep the ship."

"Aye, sir," said I, not letting a thing show.

"I don't see," he said, "as there's any necessity as to which of us takes which post."

"No, sir," I said. "Nor do I."

"D'you want to lead the shore party, then?"

" 'Tis your decision, sir."

"Do it, then. As senior, my first responsibility is the ship. And besides. . . ."

He didn't finish the sentence, but then I don't suppose he had to. We both knew as I was better at this sort of affair. Hasty Bernie was twice the seaman I was, and a finer hand with the sextant and chart than ever our poor dead captain could have hoped to be, but he weren't quite as fond of improvisation, nor as quick with a cutlass, as I was.

So I was glad of the duty because I thought I'd a better chance of pulling it off—but at the same time, I reckoned that chance to be pretty pissing poor, and I'd have been fair relieved if Bernie had taken it upon himself.

I went to the rail and looked over the men I'd be leading. There was Peter Long, and Black Eddie, and Ez Carter, and Goodman Richard—I'd no complaints about who was there and who wasn't, save that Doc Brewer might come in handy. He was nowhere to be seen, though, and I decided against sending for him. Instead I made a little speech.

"All right, boys," said I. "The Captain's gone and gotten us into another one, and we'll just have to get ourselves out. I'll tell you what it's about on the way, not that I know meself."

And then we were climbing up the ropes to the cave mouth, and I was trying to think if there was anything more I should have brought, besides the lantern, and matches, and the cutlass, and the brace of pistols, and the powder and shot, and the dagger, and the sack of biscuit, and the flask of rum, and the fifty feet of line, and the cosh in my pocket.

A little gold might have been nice, in case any bribery

were called for. I had three shillings in my purse, and that was all.

Well, it didn't seem worth going back for.

The caves were dark as the Dungeon Pits on Little Hengist until I got the lantern going. Then I had to remember the route without the Captain leading the way, which took me a little bit of a moment.

I managed it, though, with only the one wrong turning, and despite what he said to me between oaths, I swear that Black Eddie's foot was still a good ten feet from the brink of the pit when I realized we'd have done better to have turned left than right at the big pillar.

We came out in the palace wine cellar and stopped to catch our breath and look the matter over.

"Well, now," I said. "Here we are in the palace, and ahead is the stairway to the kitchens, and from there we're to find Madame Lee. Being the hour that it is, I'm thinking she'll be in her chamber. Now, where would that be?"

Black Eddie and Peter and the others stared at me like as if I'd just ordered them hanged.

"Don't you *know*?" Peter asked.

"There's no need to be takin' that tone with me, Peter Long," I told him. "No, the fact is I *don't* know. How would I? Nor would any man aboard the ship, for that matter."

"Any man, no," Good Richard pointed out. "But what about the women? Or Jamie?"

I didn't think Miss Melissa knew even as much as I did, but I saw as how he could have a point where Jamie McPhee and Mistress Coyne were considered.

"Well, it's too late now," I said. "We're here and they're not and we've to make the best of it. Be ready, but no pistols—we don't want to rouse the whole palace. Come on, then."

I drew my cutlass and led them up the stairs with the blade naked before me, and the four of them followed at my heel with their own swords out.

At the top we gathered tight together whilst I worked

the latch, and then the door opened and we all tumbled out into the kitchens, blades at the ready.

There were two people there, a man and a girl, and I judged them to be the palace baker and either his assistant or a scullery girl. Ez and Peter ran up to them and had steel at their throats in a trice.

I put down my lantern, but kept my sword ready as I walked over, a bit more leisurely than Ez and Peter had. I tried to behave as if I burst into places like this an hour before dawn, taking prisoners, as a regular thing.

"Tell us truth and no harm will come to you," I said.

They said not a word, but just cowered there, mouths agape. I took it for acceptance.

"Where is Madame Lee's chamber, then, and how do we get there from here?" I demanded.

The baker, if such he was, looked at me with even greater astonishment, but the scullery girl piped up, "It's in the north wing. You cross the hall to the stairs, go up two flights, and around, and then down the corridor to the right, and it's the last door on the right."

A fine girl, that—would blab anything to anyone. "Thank you, lass," I said, and then I looked the situation over and felt some misdoubt about it.

If we left these two free, they might raise the alarm. If we bound them, they might be found—and besides, I thought we might need all the rope we had for other uses.

"Eddie," I said. "You stay here and watch these two, and make sure neither of them tells a soul we're about."

Eddie opened his mouth to say something, most probably to protest being asked this, but then he took another look at the girl and changed his mind. "Aye aye, Billy," he said.

"Good, then. You others, come along, and try to be quiet about it."

With that, I led them along the course the lass had described.

We crossed the hall and found the stairs, climbed the stairs and found the corridor, and then we stopped, for the

wench hadn't mentioned that a guard was posted outside
the door of Madame Lee's chamber.

And what was worse, he saw us before we saw him.

I was wavering there between giving it all up as a botch
and fleeing back down the stairs, or charging ahead, since
we did outnumber him four to one and perhaps if we were
quick we could convince him not to rouse the palace, when
he called in a loud whisper, "*There* you are! My Lord,
you're two hours late!"

I blinked at him, and then grinned, and I led the lads
down the passage. I saw Ez Carter sheathe his sword, but
the rest of us kept ours ready.

"Hurry up," the guard hissed. "My relief is due soon,
and nobody bribed *him*."

We scurried up to the door beside him, and none of us
had said a word yet.

"What kept you?" he asked me. "And where's your
captain?"

"The Captain had a bit of a mishap," I said. "A whack
on the head. He's in his bunk aboard ship."

"Is he all right, then?"

"Oh, as right as he'll ever be," said I, which was true
after a fashion.

He nodded, and then he took a glance at a window at
the end of the corridor, which I had not until that moment
noticed. "The wagon's ready?" he asked.

"Um," said I, and I heard Ez Carter swearing under
his breath.

The guard insisted, "Is the wagon below the window
there, ready to catch her?"

"Well, no," I admitted. "If the truth be known, it's
not. We had a little mishap—the same one as hit the captain on the head, do you see."

At the least, I thought, now I knew what the wagon had
been intended for.

The sentry looked disconcerted, as if he'd just seen a
tax collector smile, but before he could say anything more

the bedchamber door opened and a woman's head thrust out, long hair hanging free, not decently put up.

"What're the lot of you doing here whispering outside my door at this hour?" she said.

Good was the first of us to react. He dropped his sword and grabbed for her, and caught her round the neck with one arm and pulled her out into the hallway. She was a tall wench, and thin, with hair the color of mahogany, and I thought me I knew the face from somewhere. She wore a black nightdress trimmed with lace, a pretty thing, and clearly not meant to be seen in public. When Good Richard laid hold of her her arms flew up to either side, and she made a noise like a spitting cat.

And Goodman Richard shriveled down away from her, and was turned into a toad, right before our eyes.

Whilst the rest of us were still staring, Ez Carter caught her across the back of her head with a belaying pin he'd had in his belt, and witch or no witch, she went down in a heap.

"That's her?" I asked the guard.

He nodded, staring.

I had me a thought, wagon or no wagon. I took a quick few steps to the window at the end of the passageway and looked out.

I could see all of Collyport from there, spread out before me, and the harbor beyond. The warehouse fire had died down some, but still glowed orange. All the same, I could see that some of the ships had put back into port; the *Armistead Castle* was back at her berth, but I couldn't put names to the others.

I looked down, then, to where a wagon might have waited, if we'd have had one.

Sure enough, there was a road down there—but it was a hundred feet down, and the wall was sheer stone.

The captain might have planned to take Madame Lee out that way, but I wasn't about to try it. I'd brought rope, but not enough, and I hadn't brought any tackle to secure it. Nor did I know where the road went, and men on foot, carrying a woman, would be slower and more likely to attract notice than a freight wagon would have been.

We'd have to go back out the way we came—for one thing, aside from the rest, we'd left Black Eddie in the kitchen. I turned back.

"Come on, then, this way," I called to the others, snatching up the toad and tucking it in my pocket with one hand whilst my other retrieved Good's cutlass. "Pick her up between you and come along!"

"Wait!" the guard called, "You can't . . . You owe me five guineas for this!" With a start, I remembered Captain Dancy's last words. I also remembered the three shillings in my pocket and frowned. "And besides," the man continued. "When they find me. . . ."

Ez Carter gave me a look, and I nodded. He let go his side of the woman, and while Peter Long hoisted her up across his shoulder, Ez walked up and whacked the guard soundly across the pate with his belaying pin.

He sat down suddenly against the wall, and a moment later, when I glanced back from the corner, I saw him reach up to rub his head. I could see the lump from there.

We none of us worried about him; with an eye on the witch, who was already beginning to stir, we ran for the kitchens.

Black Eddie was waiting, with the baker and the maid. The baker had his hands tied behind him and was perched on a stool, facing a wall; the wench wasn't tied at all.

"Come on," I told Eddie, and he buttoned his pants and came on. The girl got to her feet and looked around, and at the sight of Madame Lee her eyes widened.

"Maybe we'd best bring her along," Eddie suggested.

"Please yourself," I told him, not caring to waste time arguing. "As long as she doesn't slow us down."

He grabbed her wrist, and Ez grabbed the lantern, and we all trampled down the stairs to the wine cellars, Ez first, then Peter with Madame Lee over his shoulder, then me, and then Black Eddie, dragging his girl along by her wrist.

I saw as how leaving the baker as we had meant that the secret route through the caves would be a secret no more, but I didn't see any way that could be helped, since we'd no wagon outside the window to escape in, as the captain's plan had called for, and I'd no stomach for killing the baker in cold blood. A corpse in the kitchen might well tell the tale in any case.

Madame Lee raised her head from Peter's shoulder and looked at me, and I began to wonder what flies tasted like.

"Madame," I called, with my best manner. "Before you act rashly, remember there are four of us left, and if you enchant another, the rest will kill you in self-defense." I lifted the cutlass that was still in my hand. "We mean you no harm, I promise."

I was none too certain that cold steel would kill a witch as easily as that, but I hoped.

And I was more certain than ever that I knew that face, though with the long hair flying loose about it, and all of us bouncing giddily down the stairs, I couldn't place it just then.

We reached the bottom and ran through the cellars, through the door into the caves, where we found ourselves in gloom relieved by only the single lantern. It seemed worse, somehow, than it had on the way in. I looked, and saw the glass was a trifle smoked, as the wick needed trimming. I wished I'd brought more than the one, as we'd no way to trim the wick there.

Well, a man can't think of everything, and we had the one, and it was still enough to see by. I tucked the cutlass in my belt—I had two there now, my own and Goodman Richard's. "This way," I said.

"Mr. Jones," Peter said. "Might I put her down for a moment? Or could someone else carry her?"

"Is she heavy?" Ez asked.

"Not so you'd notice," Peter said. "But it's awkward, carrying a woman about that way, all on one side."

"I can walk," Madame Lee said, and she raised her

head again, and when I saw her face in the lantern light and heard that throaty voice again, I recognized her at last.

"Oh, my good Lord in heaven, and all the saints and angels," I said, staring. "It's the Caliburn Witch herself."

7.

SHE BLINKED at me, and then smiled like a cat stretches. "Billy Jones," she said. "You've a few more grey hairs than when last we met, haven't you?"

"By God I do," I agreed. "And you're the cause of a few of them!"

She just smiled at me again as Peter set her on her feet.

"You've sworn not to harm us," I told her. "For as long as Jack Dancy lives, you're sworn not to touch a single man of the *Bonny Anne*'s crew."

"Well do I know it," she answered, still smiling. "And where *is* Captain Dancy?"

"Aboard ship," I said. "He's feeling poorly."

The smile winked out like a blown candle flame.

"My Jack?" she said. "My Jack's ill?"

"I'll say no more," I told her. "It's not my place."

The other men were staring. Ez and Peter hadn't yet joined the crew six years before, when we'd tangled with the Witch; Eddie hadn't gotten a good look at her face in the dash down the cellar stairs, and hadn't been in the passageway when she came out of her room. And poor Good, of course, was a toad—I could feel him squirming about in my pocket—so he couldn't have said anything if he recognized her.

They'd all heard of the Caliburn Witch, though. Everyone in the islands had heard of the Caliburn Witch. Sometimes we'd wondered why none had heard anything *new* of her these past few years.

In a way, though, dangerous as she was, I was glad to see her there, for she *had* sworn not to harm us, and wouldn't likely flee at the first chance. We might not need Doc Brewer's geas at all.

And of course, against the likes of her, the best geas Emmanuel Brewer could concoct might not be any more use than trying to bail the ocean dry with my hat. The Caliburn Witch was not to be held lightly.

It occurred to me that Captain Dancy hadn't known which witch he'd been sent after, or he'd not have bothered about a geas. That was something that might bear a little more thought when I had time.

Just then, though, the toad in my pocket was still squirming, and that squirm reminded me. I pulled Good out of my pocket and held him out. "Can you change him back now, if you please? You *did* swear not to harm him."

She smiled that cat-smile again. "Surely I swore that, but I don't see that he's been harmed. He looks a fine, fat, healthy toad to me."

I frowned at her. "I'd reckon it harm to turn a man to a toad, and I think so would the captain. He's lost the use of his voice, hasn't he? Don't you reckon that as harm?"

She shrugged. "It might be said so," she admitted. "Alas, I can't turn him back here and now. I keep a spell ready to hand at night, against just such as you, but I'd never any need before for the cure, and I haven't got it with me."

I was about to argue, when Eddie said, "Billy, shouldn't we be getting back to the ship?" He pointed at the lantern, which was burning low and smoking more than ever.

I looked, and saw that he had a sound argument. "Come on, then," I said, tucking the toad away, and we wound our way back through the caverns to the sea.

I feared we might have to tie the Witch up and lower her down hand over hand, but she gave us no trouble about scampering down the lines, as if climbing ropes were something she did every day between the Governor's audiences.

Then again, for all I knew she might have been able to fly down, but she didn't.

The kitchen wench rode down pickaback on Black Eddie, arms about his neck and legs about his waist, and he damn near lost his hold a time or two on account of the added weight.

At the last, though, we were all down safely and back aboard the *Bonny Anne*, and the moment I came up the side, bringing up the rear as befit my position in command of the party, Hasty Bernie gave the order to up anchor and take us back to Collyport.

He was safe up on the quarterdeck, seeing to the ship, and the rest of my party was scattering to their posts in the rigging, whilst I found myself on the halfdeck with the four females.

"Which one is Madame Lee?" Miss Melissa asked, puzzled, though how she could think a lass as young as that serving maid could be the Governor's wife of five years I don't know. Governor Lee had his faults, but I'd never heard any say pedophilia was one of them.

"Who's that?" Mistress Coyne demanded, jabbing her thumb at Eddie's wench.

"Mistress Coyne!" the girl said, staring at the Governor's woman, "What are *you* doing here?"

"Who are *these* two?" asked the Caliburn Witch suspiciously.

I sighed, and tried to decide where to begin.

A croak from my pocket decided me.

"Madame Lee," I said, "allow me to present Mistress Melissa Dewhurst, who's aboard the *Bonny Anne* at Captain Dancy's personal invitation."

The two women glared at one another, but before either could speak I turned to the next. "And Mistress Annabelle Coyne," I said, "who came aboard to assist us in certain matters, and who had the misfortune to be caught on board when a fire on the docks compelled us to depart.''

She smiled graciously at Madame Lee, though with a little more tooth showing than might be strictly necessary.

"And I'm afraid," I said, "that I didn't catch the name of the young lady who came aboard with Black Eddie."

"Susan Bowditch," said the wench, and she dropped a curtsy.

"Mistress Bowditch," I said with a bow. "Welcome aboard. And you, too, Madame Lee, of course."

Madame Lee paid me no heed. She was staring at Mistress Coyne with that cat-smile on her face again. I'd never seen it until an hour or so before, but already I was growing sore weary of that expression.

"I begin," she said, "to understand. Rouse Jack Dancy out here, I've something to tell him."

I exchanged a glance with Miss Melissa.

"I'll see if he's to be roused," Miss Melissa said, and she turned away and trotted to the cabin.

The ship was heeling over as we rounded the Seal Stones, and I could see Mistress Coyne shifting as she tried to keep her balance. Poor little Susan Bowditch had to grab for the rail, and I guessed she'd be seasick soon.

The Witch, of course, didn't notice. It would take more than a ship's motion to bother *her*.

"Ladies," I began, thinking we might go below, and then I stopped.

I couldn't take them down to the cabin, not with the captain's corpse still stretched out there. The wardroom that I shared with Bernie was hardly a fit place for them, the fo'c'sle even worse. The black, airless depths of the hold would hardly be an improvement.

The gundeck, perhaps?

I decided we'd do best to stay where we were.

I looked about. The sky was lightening in the east; Bernie had a good lot of canvas spread, and we were making way nicely. I judged we'd be back in Collyport within an hour, if the wind didn't turn foul.

An hour on deck in such mild weather would do no harm.

"Excuse me for a moment, ladies," said I, and I trotted over to the starboard shrouds, where Black Eddie had just descended to the deck.

"Eddie," I said, "what were you thinking of, bringing the wench along?"

"I'm sorry, Billy," he said. "She just got the better of me for a moment."

"Will it trouble you any if we put her ashore when we make port?" I asked.

He thought about that for a moment. "She's a pretty little thing," he said. "But I suppose it'd be best."

That was one problem solved—and as I watched Mistress Bowditch lurch against the rail and spew over the side, I didn't doubt that she'd want to be put off the ship.

I knew what the wagon had been for, now—that was another problem solved. The captain had meant for us to come in through the caves, but go out through the window, so that the route in would remain a secret, safe for later use. He'd probably have told the baker that we crept in earlier and hid in the wine cellars.

And we'd done what the Governor wanted—another problem gone.

Now there were just three more that I saw left to us.

First, now that we had the Witch aboard, what were we to *do* with her?

Second, how were we to keep her from discovering that Jack Dancy was dead, and that her oath not to harm us was thereby void? She'd sworn long ago that the *Bonny Anne* and all aboard would be hers when Jack Dancy died.

And third, what was the parrot for?

Well, I judged that solutions would either present themselves or not, and in the meanwhile there were things to be done.

I glanced over, and saw Mistress Coyne and Madame Lee exchanging words, and with them looks meant to freeze the heart. Little Susan Bowditch was still sick at the rail.

And here came Miss Melissa back again.

"My apologies, Madame Lee," she said. "But the captain's in no state to be seen, nor will he be for some time yet."

The Witch gave a smile worse than any I'd yet seen on her face, and I thought my heart would stop.

"Mistress Dewhurst," she said. "I've seen Jack Dancy at his worst."

Miss Melissa threw me a puzzled and angry look, and I told her, "Madame Lee once held the captain prisoner for a fortnight, six years ago."

The Witch grinned. Jack Dancy had been her prisoner, right enough—but not in the dungeons with the rest of us.

I could see that Miss Melissa didn't know what to make of that, but she could hardly ask for explanations just then. "All the same," she said, facing up to the Witch with a courage I didn't know she had, "Aboard his own ship, he'll not be seen at his worst."

I tried to distract them all by saying, "Mistress Coyne, we'll be back in port shortly, and we'll be sending you ashore there."

She was about to reply when a cry came from the masthead, "Sail ho!"

We all looked up, and I called, "Where away?"

"Dead ahead!" came the reply.

We looked, and sure enough, there was a frigate rounding the point ahead, just where we'd been headed. We were closing on her quickly, and she was turning broadside to, rather than continuing on her course. She was scarce a quarter mile away—the headlands had hidden her—and we were bearing down on her.

"What colors?" Hasty Bernie called from the quarter-deck.

"She's flying the Governor's flag," came the reply. "She's the *Armistead Castle*!"

That was all right, then—we all knew the *Armistead*

Castle. We'd seen her in port that night, seen her ahead of us when we put out to sea, and I'd seen her back at her moorings from the palace window. She was the Governor's own ship that he called out to chase away any pirates foolish enough to venture into Collyport without his permission, and as we were on the Governor's business, so to speak, we'd naught to fear from her.

We were just beginning to relax when she opened fire.

8.

IT WASN'T a full broadside, just a warning shot, but the ball whistled overhead and scared the bloody hell out of us all.

"What the hell?" I asked, and that was the mildest remark I heard on that deck. Miss Melissa and Mistress Coyne said far worse; Madame Lee and Mistress Bowditch didn't bother with words.

"Heave to!" Bernie called, and the men hurried to obey, while the women and I stood there amidships, all of them talking at once, trying to figure out what was happening.

"Hail her," Bernie ordered the man at the masthead, but the lookout called down, "They're lowering a boat!"

That meant a parley, I judged.

I began to have an idea what was happening. I couldn't be sure, though, and I thought I'd best cover every possibility I could. I pulled the rope from my waist, that line I'd taken into the caves and not used.

"Your pardon, ladies," I said, and I proceeded to bind their hands behind them—first Madame Lee, and then Mistress Coyne, and just to be sure I went on and tied Mistress Bowditch and Miss Melissa, as well.

Miss Melissa started to protest, but I whispered, "Bear with me, Mistress, please."

She shrugged and let me tie her hands.

Then I drew one of the two cutlasses on my belt and waited for the parley boat to arrive.

A few minutes later—which seemed like half of eternity—the boat bumped up against the side. A couple of the men secured it, and Peter Long, who was one of them, called, "Officer coming aboard, Mr. Jones!" As the officer's cocked hat appeared in the entry port, I lifted the sword to Madame Lee's throat.

The man's face was shocked, when he saw me standing there behind a row of women, all with their hands bound, and one with my blade against her neck.

"My Lord, man," he began, and then stopped.

"Speak your piece," I told him. "Why'd you fire on us?"

He blinked, and then said, "I'm here at the Governor's orders, sir. He'd heard that the crew of the *Bonny Anne* had abducted an innocent woman from Collyport, one Mistress Annabelle Coyne, and he came down to the port and sent us out after you."

I blinked back at him, much relieved. The Governor hadn't double-crossed us, then, and wasn't going to sink us for kidnapping his wife. Instead, he'd thought we were double-crossing *him*, and stealing the wrong woman.

"Governor Lee's aboard your ship?" I asked.

"Yes, sir, he is," the officer replied.

"Well, then, you can tell him he's been misinformed. Mistress Coyne was not kidnapped; she came aboard of her own free will, and she's free to go, any time she chooses." I turned the cutlass about and used it to cut the cords on Mistress Coyne's wrists. Then I cut Mistress Bowditch's, as well—this was as good a time as any to get her out of the way. I pushed them both toward the officer. "Here she is," I said. "And another as well, and you're welcome to take them back with you."

The officer stammered for a moment, and then asked Mistress Bowditch, "You're Annabelle Coyne?"

"No," Mistress Coyne said angrily, "*I* am."

Mistress Bowditch was still too seasick to say anything; she just nodded.

"And those other two?" the Governor's man asked, pointing.

"Spoils of war," I said. "And none of your concern."

I thought that the Witch would betray me, and I think for a moment she thought so, too, but instead she grinned.

"They don't speak English," I added.

The Witch nodded eagerly. Miss Melissa glowered at me, but kept silent.

The officer—a lieutenant, he was, by his uniform—looked about, and then decided to take what he was given and see what happened. "This way, ladies," he said, and he helped Mistress Coyne and Mistress Bowditch down over the side.

Then the boat pulled away, and Miss Melissa shouted, "Get those ropes off me!"

Madame Lee didn't say a word, but the ropes fell away from her wrists.

I set to untying Miss Melissa, and spoke up cheerfully. "There, now, ladies, we've settled that! We're rid of those two, who would have been nothing but trouble, and we still have you. I take it from your silence, Ma'am, that you had no particular wish to be sent aboard the *Armistead Castle*?"

I looked at Madame Lee, and she looked back.

"Mr. Jones," she said, "I've known for some time that my husband was tired of my company, and I've no more love for him. I enjoyed playing the Governor's lady and being mistress of Collyport, but it's not worth the grief if he's going to such extremes as this to get rid of me!"

My mouth fell open.

She sneered—a harsh word to use of a lady, but she did. "Come now," she said. "Did you think I didn't know, when I saw Annabelle Coyne on this deck, that it was

George Lee who had sent you to kidnap me? And furthermore, do you think I didn't know why? He's trying to rid himself of two problems at once—Jack Dancy and myself. Jack didn't know who I was, but my dear Georgie did. So he sent you to capture me, and Jack agreed, thinking he could handle an ordinary witch—Doc Brewer's surely prepared a little spell of some sort! But then Jack was to find himself with no mere hedgerow enchantress, but the infamous Caliburn Witch aboard, the same who he had scarcely escaped six years ago. Georgie knew I'd rather stay aboard the *Bonny Anne* with my Jack than in his palace with him, and he was right!''

''*Your* Jack!'' Miss Melissa burst out.

''Aye,'' the witch told her. ''*My* Jack, or he was once, at any rate, and long before he was *your* lover. But what's it matter now that he's dead?''

My mouth fell open, and Miss Melissa's snapped shut.

''Dead?'' she said.

''How did you know?'' I asked—for I knew better than to lie any more to the Caliburn Witch.

She gave me a bitter smile. ''I know my Jack,'' she said. ''If there was still breath in his body, he'd have come on deck when someone fired on his *Bonny Anne*.''

We could scarce argue with that, for it was the plain truth.

''How did it happen?'' the Witch asked.

''He slipped and hit his head,'' I said. ''In the alley behind Old Joe's Tavern.''

Her eyes widened. ''Is that all? It wasn't the Black Sorcerer? Nor Bartholomew Sanchez? Nor the Pundit of Oul?''

''No,'' I said. ''Just a fall and a broken neck.''

She shook her head.

It was at that moment that the frigate fired a full broadside at us.

The roar swept over us, and the balls tore through the rigging; I heard lines snap and canvas tear and shot howl through the air. We all spun in astonishment.

"Man the guns!" Hasty Bernie cried from the quarter-deck, and men swarmed to the gundeck.

"What?" the Witch cried. "He *dares*?"

"Dares what?" I shouted back over the pounding feet and the rattling of the gun tackles. "Who?"

"That worm who called me his wife! That little bitch from the kitchens told him I was aboard, and now he means to sink us!"

"How do you. . . ." I started to ask, but then I remembered who I spoke to. Instead I asked, "Why didn't he just sail away?"

"And let everyone aboard his ship know he was leaving his lady in Jack Dancy's hands? He couldn't do that. How could he ever hold his head up again if he sailed away and left his own wife in the hands of an adventurer like Jack Dancy?"

"But then why didn't he send a boat to parley. . . ." I began.

"You bloody *fool*!" she shrieked, turning on me, just as the frigate's second broadside thundered out at us, "He doesn't want me back, he wants me *dead*! He's trying to sink us! He can't just sail away, but if I die accidentally in the fight, who's to say he's done wrong? And die I might—even a witch can drown in twenty fathoms of salt water!"

I heard the crunch of a ball hitting the side, and saw a fore mainsail sheet flying free where a shot had snapped it, and then our own guns roared out, raggedly. Doc Brewer tottered up from below, the canvas bag of unused arcana in his fist, looking about wildly.

I knew we had no chance; the *Bonny Anne* carried eighteen guns to the frigate's thirty-two, and smaller guns at that. We had scarce thirty seamen aboard, what with having left port so hurriedly, while he surely had two hundred. "Strike!" I called to Bernie. "He can't sink us if we strike! Better a dungeon than drowning!"

"NO!" shrieked the Witch. She staggered across the

deck and snatched the bag from Doc Brewer, then tore it open.

She looked up at me with a grin of triumph on her face, and snatched out something long and thin and yellowish. She lifted it above her head, stretched between her two hands, and shouted out something.

What she shouted was in no language I had ever heard before, nor any I ever wish to hear again.

The frigate's third broadside roared out, but when I looked at the Governor's ship I saw that it had heeled back, and that most of the balls would pass over us, too high to do any damage.

And our own ship was heeling back, as well, and the sea between us seemed to be rising up, and I tried to guess what trick of the tide or the gunfire could cause that, and then I realized it wasn't any natural trick at all.

The wave rose up higher and higher, above the level of our decks, and then still higher, above the spars; the frigate was hidden from sight now behind a rising wall of surging green water.

The Witch was standing, arms raised and spread, like a statue; wind whipped her hair about her as if she stood in a hurricane, but elsewhere the air was almost dead calm now, the sails hanging limp. Her eyes blazed with a green fire.

The water rose up until it seemed to cover half the sky—and then it fell.

On the frigate.

The backwash sent the *Bonny Anne* rocking and bouncing, yawing wildly, and I grabbed for the rail, and saw others doing the same—everyone but the Witch herself grabbed for a handhold somewhere.

Spray burst up over the side and caught me in the face.

When I was able to clear my eyes and look again, there was no trace of the *Armistead Castle* anywhere, only the rocks and the tossing waves.

The sea calmed gradually, and I heard Bernie sending the men to repair the damage we'd taken in the battle. I didn't concern myself with that; instead I paid attention only to the Caliburn Witch.

The light had faded from her eyes, and she lowered the yellowish thing and tossed it to Doc Brewer. I finally got a decent look at it, and saw that it was the skeleton of an eel.

"*That* should teach the man not to mistreat his wife!" the Witch snapped. She turned. "Mr. Abernathy!" she called. "Set a course for Drummond Isle; we'll be putting Mistress Dewhurst ashore there, in her home town!"

Miss Melissa started when she heard that, and glanced at the Witch, but didn't say anything.

"Aye aye," Bernie called back, in a puzzled tone.

I was just as puzzled. "Your pardon, ma'am," I ventured. "But what is it you're planning?"

I remembered well how, six years before, she had sworn to see me and my mates dead.

So did she, I judged.

Was she planning to set Miss Melissa ashore first, and then sink us, or burn us?

Such scruples hardly seemed likely, given that she'd had no hesitation in sending Mistress Coyne and Mistress Bowditch to the bottom, along with everyone else aboard the *Armistead Castle*. True, Mistress Coyne had been her husband's mistress, and Mistress Bowditch had tattled to the Governor, but Miss Melissa was her dead lover's woman, so she'd grounds for a grudge there, too.

"Well, Mr. Jones," she said, turning back to me with the least malicious smile I'd yet seen on her face. "I've had my fill of the Governor's Palace, and for that matter all of Collyport. I'd seen all I cared to of Caliburn Island five years ago, or I'd not have left it. I think the time has come to roam a little, to wander about—and it seems to me that a ship and crew have just fallen into my hands that would suit me fine for that wandering. There's the little matter of your deaths, yours and a dozen others, a sentence I handed down back on Caliburn six years ago. Well, I'm willing to commute that sentence to a few years of penal servitude—aboard this ship, under my command.'' She made the smile into another of her cat-grins. ''Or I could hang you. It's your choice, Mr. Jones.''

It took me no time to decide *that* one. ''Aye aye, Captain Lee,'' I replied, saluting.

We put Melissa Dewhurst and five crewmen who asked ashore on Drummond Isle eleven days later, where for all I know they're all living peacefully to this day. John Hastings Abernathy, who after all had never angered the Witch and hadn't been with us those six years before, was retired three months after, and put ashore in Collyport, where he took a post with the new Acting Governor as portmaster. I was promoted to first mate.

Captain Dancy we gave a fine burial at sea the very afternoon after the sinking of the *Armistead Castle*. Captain Lee turned the toad back into Goodman Richard, using Doc Brewer's paraphernalia, that same night.

As for the rest, Captain Lee says she'll set us free when she grows bored. She's no worse a master than was Jack Dancy, for the most part, and as she's taken a fancy to me I've no need now to wait until we're in port to find a woman to share my bunk.

Like most of Captain Dancy's plans, the whole affair had all worked out well enough, if not the way we expected.

I see how it was meant to work—the fire for a distraction, the entry through the caves, the escape in the wagon below the window, the geas to hold the Witch under control until we could put her ashore somewhere. Captain Dancy hadn't planned to have Mistress Coyne aboard, nor to have the Governor think that Mistress Coyne had chosen Jack Dancy over himself and come out to get her back. He hadn't known that Madame Lee was no ordinary witch, but the Caliburn Witch.

It's pretty much all clear now.

But we never did find out what the damn parrot was for.

Coming in hardcover from Tor Books in 1993:

SPLIT HEIRS

by **Lawrence Watt-Evans**
and **Esther Friesner**

*The ultimate saga
of flashing swords, high magic,
and hopeless dynastic confusion!*

Turn the page for a special preview—

"THREE?"

The scream from the north tower of the Palace of Divinely Tranquil Thoughts was loud and shrill enough to shatter seven stained-glass windows in the banqueting hall below—six of them among the handful of remaining works by the master artisan Oratio, dating from some fourteen centuries back, and the last a cheap imitation installed during the reign of Corulimus the Decadent, a mere millennium ago.

As shards of glass rattled across the table King Gudge, Lord of Hydrangea, looked up from his wine at the sudden influx of daylight and growled, "What in the name of the five ways to gut an ox was *that*?"

Trembling at his royal master's elbow, Lord Polemonium replied, "I think—I *think*, Your Omnipotent and Implacable Majesty, that it is the ebullient and convivial exultation of Her Most Complacent Highness, Queen Artemisia, your connubial helpmeet, as she experiences the transitory distress of parturition, preparatory to the imminent joy attending the nativity of your supremely longed-for progeny."

King Gudge plucked a sliver of blue glass from his goblet and munched it thoughtfully as he considered this reply. Then he drew his sword Obliterator and lopped off Lord Polemonium's head, adding to the mess on the table.

"Now, let's give that another go-around, all right?" the king said, wiping the gory blade clean on the lace tablecloth as he gazed at his remaining ministers. "I'll ask one more time: What was *that*?"

"The queen's having the baby," said Lord Filaree, with all dispatch, watching Lord Polemonium's head. It was still bouncing.

"Oh." King Gudge thrust Obliterator back into its scabbard and picked up his wine. "About time." He swilled down the measure, getting most of it in the black tangle of his beard.

Farther down the table, out of earshot and swordreach, Lord Croton nudged Lord Filaree in the ribs. "Is it just me, or did our royal lady holler 'Three'?"

Lord Filaree shrugged, not really paying any attention to the question. Every time he was "invited" to one of King Gudge's council meetings/drinking parties, he only had eyes and ears for His Majesty. It might have been the same sort of morbid fascination that made commoners stop and stare at a particularly gruesome cart-wreck, or perhaps just the fact that any minister caught *not* having eyes and ears for King Gudge alone wound up not having eyes and ears.

"I said," Lord Croton repeated testily, "why would she scream 'three'?"

"Maybe she and her handmaid are playing a round of gorf," Lord Filaree hazarded without turning.

Lord Croton snorted quietly. "Filaree, the correct gorfing cry is 'five on the loo'ard side and mind the pelicans!' Any fool knows that. Besides, pregnant women never play gorf."

"My dear Croton, you know how these women are when they're giving birth. They say all sorts of nonsense. Didn't your own wife—?" He let the question hang unfinished.

"Well, yes," Lord Croton confessed. "While she was in travail, my darling Ione called me a bubble-headed, lust-crazed, self-indulgent, slavering babboon. And she swore I'd never lay a hand on her again as long as I lived. Which was not going to be too much longer because she was going to kill me as soon as she got her strength back. All very well, Filaree, but she did not yell 'three.' "

"Well, perhaps Her Majesty has decided that our new sovereign-by-right-of-conquest already knows that he is a bubble-headed, lust-crazed, self-indulgent, slavering babboon," Lord Filaree suggested.

"*Knows* it! He'd take it as a bloody compliment."

Filaree nodded. "Indeed. Therefore, let us assume that Her Majesty is not exclaiming 'three' but 'whee!' "

" 'Whee'?" Lord Croton echoed doubtfully.

"A cry of joy denoting that her labor has been successfully accomplished and that she no longer needs to remain in isolation in the north tower, according to ancient Hydrangean tradition governing pregnant queens."

Lord Croton shook his head. "I don't know, Filaree. Now that the baby's here and she can come out of the north tower, it also means that she'll have to go back to sleeping with King Gudge. That's not the sort of thing I can picture any sane woman celebrating."

"Well, it makes a heap of a lot more sense than caterwauling *numbers*!" Lord Filaree countered. "Anyhow, why on earth would Queen Artemisia shout 'three,' tell me that!"

Lord Croton thought about it. "Right," he concluded. "No reason for it at all. 'Whee' it is. Was. Should be." He doodled on the council table a bit with his penknife for awhile, then said, "Funny, Croton; this ancient Hydrangean tradition about isolating pregnant queens—"

"Um?"

"I never heard of it."

"Three?" shrieked Queen Artemisia from the bed. "Oh merciful stars, don't tell me there's *three* of them!"

Old Ludmilla stood by the royal receiving cradle and looked helpless. "Oh, my darling lambikins, you know I'd never tell you the eentsiest thing as might trouble your dear thoughts at a time like this." The green silk-wrapped bundle in the crook of her arm began to wail. "Certainly not, not when my precious Missy-mussy has just been through such a strain, bearing up like the adorable little brave trouper that she is when other girlies would be a-weeping and a-wailing and a-carrying on something disgraceful to—"

"Three!" howled the queen. "Three, three, *three*, pox take all Gorgorians and the horses they rode in on! There is—there is most definitely—there is going to be—"

All aflutter, old Ludmilla laid the swaddled newborn in the huge, ceremonial cradle with its scarlet hangings and gold-leafed dragon headboard and hastened to her lady's bedside. "Lawks and welladay, sweet Missy-mussy, whyever are you panting so? And your face—! I do declare, it's gone the most unbecoming shade of lavender, it has. Oh, wurra-wurra and—"

"—there is going to be a third one," Queen Artemisia said with jaw taut and sweat drenching every inch of her body. *"And here it comes now!"*

Some time later, old Ludmilla lifted a beautifully formed little boy from the Basin of Harmonious Immersion—one of the oldest pieces of the Old Hydrangean royal house's childbirth accessory set—and whipped a green satin swaddling cloth around his trembling limbs before showing him to his mother.

"There, now, Missy-mussy," she said, as pleased as if she'd handled the business end of the birth herself. "All washed and neat and tidy. Isn't he a lamb?" She bore the babe to the receiving cradle in triumph, but before she laid him down in it she paused and turned to her mistress. "Ah . . . not any more coming, are there, love?"

"No," said the queen, lying pale and limp against an avalanche of overstuffed pink brocade pillows. She sounded near the brink of total exhaustion. She also sounded more than a little cranky.

Old Ludmilla cocked her head, the better to turn her one functioning ear in Queen Artemisia's direction. "Quite sure, are we?"

"We are positive," the queen returned.

"You were wrong before, you know. Of course, arithmetic never was one of your strengths. I remember saying to your dear, departed, decapitated da, King Fumitory the Twenty-Second, I said to him, 'Our Missy-mussy has her charm, but she couldn't add a wolf to a sheepfold and get lambchops.' That's what *I* said."

"And *I* say—" Queen Artemisia's clear blue eyes narrowed "—*I* say that if you call me 'Missy-mussy' one more time, I shall ask my husband—may his skull crack like an acorn under a millstone—to give me your liver roasted with garlic as a childbirth gift. What do you say to *that*?"

Ludmilla gave an indignant sniff. "I say there's some people who've grown a shade too big for their breeches, that's what. My liver roasted with garlic indeed! When you know garlic gives nursing mothers the wind something scandalous."

She placed the satin-swathed infant in the cradle and turned on her mistress in a fury. "But that's just *my* opinion, isn't it? And who am I to you, eh? Just the woman who raised you from a nasty little snippet of a royal Hydrangean princess, is all! Only the one who stood by your side on the royal city ramparts while your dear, departed, decapitated da, King Fumitory the Twenty-Second, was doing his best to fight off the invasion of those loathsome Gorgorian barbarian hordes! Merely the loyal soul who helped you hide in the royal turnip cellar after that thoroughly rude *Gudge* person did for your daddy right there in the Audience Chamber of the Sun's Hidden Face and got all that blood worked into the carpets so bad that *three* royal housekeepers have quit in disgust! Simply—"

"Three," groaned Queen Artemisia, and yanked a pillow out from under her head to slam over her face. Still from beneath the downy bolster came the pitiful, half-smothered whimper, *"Three."*

"Well . . . yes." Ludmilla pulled her tirade up on a short rein, taken back by Queen Artemisia's obvious despair. The crone cast a myopic eye over the contents of the ceremonial cradle. "And the steadfast handmaid who saw her own darling Missy-mussy give birth to three beautiful, cuddly, perfect—"

"Death sentences," said the queen, and threw the pillow at Ludmilla.

The ancient waitingwoman sighed. "I'll make the tea."

Later, as the two ladies shared a pot of well-steeped wenwort tea, Queen Artemisia recovered some of her self-possession. "They are beautiful," she admitted, gazing into the cradle at the three drowsy bundles. Ludmilla had most thoughtfully lugged the heavy piece of ceremonial furniture near Artemisia's bed so that the new mother could look at her babes in comfort. Instead of the dreamy maternal smile Ludmilla expected, the queen's expression grew stern. "Too beautiful for Gudge to sacrifice in the name of his beastly Gorgorian superstitions!"

"Ah, well, you know how these men are, dearie." Ludmilla poured more tea. "They do have their little ways. If it's not leaving all their clothes in the middle of the floor then it's believing that more than one babe at a birth means more than one father at a begetting."

"It was bad enough when I thought I was only carrying twins," Queen Artemisia said, nibbling a fortifying bit of seedcake. "It was during that savage Gorgorian holiday, the Feast of the Rutting Goat, when I started getting my insides kicked out by *two* sets of feet and hands. Three." Never again would she be able to pronounce that number without twisting her finely-featured face into the most grotesque grimace.

"I never did understand the point of the celebration," Ludmilla admitted. "Aside from giving all the apprentices a day to run around and cudgel the brains out of innocent chickens. All those ladies rushing through the streets with their biddies hanging out, waving bundles of dried ferns and cucumbers . . ."

"Women's magic." Queen Artemisia's full lip curled disdainfully. "Gorgorian women. Limited, I have learned, to minor fortune-telling skills and the occasional attempt at influencing matters of love, sex, and fertility. The male Gorgorians have absolutely no use for it, Gudge told me, but as long as it keeps their females busy and out of mischief, they *graciously* permit it."

Ludmilla sighed so deeply that the several layers of phoenix-point gold lace fluffing out the flat bosom of her gown fluttered like autumn leaves. "Oh, I do so miss them," she said.

"Miss who?"

"*Our* magic. Our wizards, I mean."

Queen Artemisia did not spare her handmaid any sympathy. "They were no use and you know it."

"Oh! My lady!" Ludmilla clapped one scrawny hand to her mouth and made a slightly complex and very silly warding sign with the other. "Such disrespect for the great, the powerful, the masters of all arcane knowledge, the gentlemen whose mystic studies have made them privy to the secrets of—"

"Privy is the word," the queen snapped. "And *to* the royal privy with them and all their useless spells and cantrips! Their magic was like a gold-dipped pig's bladder: all flash and glitter, all wind, all worthless. What good did their so-called arcane knowledge do my poor father when the Gorgorians attacked? Where were our wizards and their sorcerous weapons then?"

"Hmph!" Ludmilla's paper-thin nostrils flared indignantly. "*Some* of us know that worthwhile magic is not something you can just whistle up to do your bidding, like a sheepdog. *Some* of us know that preparations for a thaumaturgical assault of any real strategic value requires careful, one might even say *meticulous*, preparation. Why, a single wrong word, an improperly pronounced syllable, a pass of the wand from left to right, pinky extended, rather than right to left, pinky down, could mean all the difference between winning the battle and having your guts ripped out by the demons of the abyss. Throtteliar the Magnificent told me so his very own self, not twenty minutes before fleeing the palace—or trying to flee, at any rate.''

Queen Artemisia made a noise that in a person of lesser status might have been called a snort. ''So instead of anything useful,'' she said, ''our wondrous wizards pottered around with a bunch of over-refined spells that are too complex and too damned *long* to be practical, and while they were still just warming up their preliminary incantations they wound up having their heads lopped off by my royal husband, may bats nest in his ears for the winter.''

Ludmilla nodded, sighing. ''Since the wizards never did the man a lick of harm, I do wonder sometimes, why *did* he insist on executing them all?''

Queen Artemisia handed the empty teacup to her handmaid. ''You know Gudge. So do I, more's the pity. Ordinarily you'd imagine that if a thought ever managed to crawl into his skull it would die of loneliness and despair. Yet at the same time there is a certain primitive cunning to the creature. Just because our wizards weren't able to get their wands up in time to prevent his conquest of our kingdom, he still saw their powers as a possible threat for the future. My louse-ridden lord is a simple, direct, and practical man: He decided that the best way to safeguard his future was to eliminate theirs.''

''Oh my, so sad, so sad.'' Ludmilla took a purple handkerchief from her sleeve and dabbed her eyes. ''I know I shouldn't weep—the public beheadings were almost a year ago, and it does so weaken my sight—but I can't help it. It was such a moving ceremony.''

''Moving indeed,'' Queen Artemisia observed dryly. ''The way some of those wizards kept moving even after their heads were cut off was quite impressive, which was doubtless why Gudge ordered his men to round up the truant parts and burn them all. I heard that they had to chase Master Urien's head all the way to the Street of the Mushroom Vendors before they caught it and brought it back to the bonfire.''

Old Ludmilla grew more and more nostalgic and misty-eyed over the past. "Do you remember, precious lambi-kins, how beautifully Master Urien's head prophesied just before King Gudge drop-kicked it into the flames? 'Thine own downfall, O thou crawling blight of Gorgorian hon-eysuckle which doth strangle the fair and noble oak of the Hydrangean kingdom, shall spring from thine own—' " She stopped and wept afresh. "That was when your hub-bikins punted the poor thing into the fire. I think it was very rude of the king not to allow Master Urien's head to finish what it had to say."

"Then it shouldn't have called Gudge a honeysuckle," Queen Artemisia concluded. "All I remember of the whole disgusting business is that the smoke from the burning wizard-parts made me throw up. That was when I first suspected I might be pregnant." She closed her eyes and sank deeper into the pillows. "Well, what's done is done. At least I was able to keep Gudge from finding out I was *that* pregnant by making up the whole ancient Hydrangean custom of secluding the royal mother-to-be. Not that he cared." She made that same unladylike noise again. "For Gudge, women are either beddable or invisible."

"My lady," Ludmilla said softly, "shall I go ahead with the plan?"

"Yes, yes, do." Queen Artemisia's voice sounded weaker and weaker. "Only you'll have to travel with two babies instead of just one. Are you up to it? You're not as young as you used to be."

"And who is, I'd like to know?" Old Ludmilla's face was already a web of creepy wrinkles, but she carved out two more frown-lines right between the eyes as she glow-ered at the queen. It was wasted on Artemisia, whose eyes remained shut. "Don't you worry about me, I'm sure. I know my duty, even if *some* people don't know the first thing about courtesy to their good and loyal servants. I'll take the babies straightaway to your royal brother, Prince Mimulus and—"

"Weasel," came the faint comment.

"Eh?" Ludmilla cupped her good ear.

Queen Artemisia sighed faintly. "You'll never find him if you blunder around in the eastern mountains asking for Prince Mimulus. Gudge's soldiers did that for ages and came up empty-handed. The whole point of going undercover to lead the secret Old Hydrangean resistance movement is to keep everything about it a secret. You don't want Prince Mimulus of Hydrangea—"

"Don't I, then?" Ludmilla blinked in puzzlement.

"You want the Black Weasel, brave and dashing heroic leader of the Bold Bush-dwellers."

"Right, then, my poppet." Ludmilla nodded. "I go to the eastern mountains with the babies, then, and I ask around for the Black Weasel."

"The Black Weasel, *brave and dashing heroic leader of the Bold Bush-dwellers*," Artemisia corrected her. "It's no use asking for him any other way, he's given strict instructions to his followers that they are not to say one word about him to anyone who doesn't use his full title. Do you remember the first message I sent him when I suspected I was carrying twins?"

"Yes indeed, my cherub." Ludmilla smiled at the memory—not so much because it was a particularly pleasant one, but merely because it was there at all; many of her memories weren't, these days. "We had young Pringus Cattlecart run up to the mountains with it. Such a pretty laddie, Pringus!"

"Looks aren't everything," Artemisia muttered. "He forgot to ask for the Black Weasel properly, and he was still wandering from one mountain village to another when Gudge's patrol caught him. Lucky for me, the message was unsigned and in code. Unlucky for Pringus, Gudge got so annoyed when no one could translate the note that he gave the poor boy over to his Gorgorian bodyguards as their regimental . . . mascot."

"Oh." Ludmilla blanched. "Now that you mention it, the last time I saw the young man he didn't look half so cheerful as he used to. Well, never you mind, my waddleduckums, your Ludmilla will do everything right."

"Ummmm," Artemisia murmured drowsily.

"Now first off, let's see . . ." Ludmilla began to gather herself together. "Where *are* those portraits? Whoopsa-daisy, here they be, right where I left them. Dearie, rouse yourself a bit, there's a good girl. You've got to name these sweet dollykits before I go, you know. Now here's the miniature of Prince Helenium the Wise. Which one will you name for him?"

"My firstborn son," the queen replied, her voice muzzy.

"Well, and which one's that?"

"Oh, Ludmilla, the one that's not a *girl!*"

"Hmph! There's *two* of 'em as aren't girls, and as like as two straws in a haystack they are. Or haven't you been paying attention?"

Artemisia opened one cold, blue eye. "I shall pay the closest attention to your execution if you don't stop dith-ering. Didn't you tie the sacred red cord around the wrist of my firstborn?"

"Lawks! Well, I never—I am *such* a goose; of course I did. Let me just unwrap the babes a wee bit and . . . ah, there it is, red as red can be. So! I'll just untie it a moment so's I can thread this charm on the cord and we're all— Oh, it *is* a striking resemblance to Prince Helenium, isn't it?"

Prince Helenium had died two centuries ago, but con-sidering how old Ludmilla looked, it was entirely possible that they had been acquainted. She babbled on about the many virtues of the old Hydrangean prince until her royal mistress rather peevishly instructed her to get on with it. "We'll never get these babies officially named and off to safety at the rate you're going."

"Oh! Now see what you've made me do, you willful girl! I've gone and dropped the naming tokens in the cra-dle. All righty, my little dovey-byes, let's just get you all named spang-spang-spang, jig time, like you was no bet-ter than a litter of puppies."

Ludmilla was in a full-blown snit. Artemisia fought to

open both eyes in time to watch her handmaid fussing about in the ceremonial cradle, muttering darkly as she worked. "*You* are Prince Helenium, and *you* can just be called after Lord Helianthus the Lawgiver, and never you mind about the proper naming rituals! No, we're in a *hurry*, we are! Now where did I put the cord for tying your token 'round your little wristy—? Ah, here it is. I'll be forgetting where I put my own head next, we're so desperate *quick* about things! And *you*, you can be named for Queen Avena the Well-Beloved—oh, bother these slip-knots, I never could tie a decent . . . *there*! Fine. Done. All tagged with their proper tokens and with no more observance of the decencies than was they three sacks full of grain for the market. Will there be anything else, Your Majesty?"

Icicles hung from Ludmilla's last words, but Artemisia was too tired to mind. "Just change into your disguise and take Avena and Helianthus to my brother. And let me get some rest before I strangle you," said the queen as she drifted off into a well-deserved sleep.

Protocols for Military Personnel in the Service of the Ancient & Honorable Kingdom of the Hydrangeans

1. A soldier is a gentleman, and will comport himself, or in those special cases where female personnel may be employed in the armed forces, herself, as a gentleman—or, as the case may be, a lady. While a certain degree of aggressive physical activity may be required in the performance of a Hydrangean soldier's duties, this in no way implies that he or she shall at any time behave in a rude, thoughtless, or impious manner. (See Volume 1, Articles 15 through 224, for further commentary on appropriate behavior.)

2. The Hydrangean soldier will at all times, while on duty, (con't.)

Code of the Gorgorian Warrior

First Rule: Do what your war leader tells you.

Second Rule: Don't ask questions.

Third Rule: When in doubt, kill it.